Viva Cristo Rey

Viva Cristo Rey

Gil Sanchez

authorHOUSE®

AuthorHouse™
1663 Liberty Drive
Bloomington, IN 47403
www.authorhouse.com
Phone: 1-800-839-8640

Published by AuthorHouse   03/28/2012

ISBN: 978-1-4670-6869-7 (sc)
ISBN: 978-1-4670-6868-0 (hc)
ISBN: 978-1-4670-6867-3 (e)

Library of Congress Control Number: 2011918722

Early spring in the Del Rey community of Detroit, the young priest sat on the porch at his grandmother's house looking through damaged, faded photographs, his mind imprisoned in each of the moments. The photos were of his family, all of them dead now. It seemed that each photo called out to him. He looked up at a brand-new 1937 Chevrolet passing by, as it whipped up some dead leaves left over from last year. His thoughts quickly fell back to the people in Europe and to maniacs in black and brown uniforms with evil stares on their faces as they shot innocent people down; killings, destruction, all of it played out in a horror sequence in his mind, none of it making any sense. He questioned why and silently pleaded for some directions from God. His faded memories of his parents were happy ones, but dark clouded nightmares had hidden many of his recollections, most of his adolescence had been stored away, lost somewhere in time.

His bachelor's degree was in sociology at Holy Cross Seminary. The young father studied and researched how humanity could, on the one hand, produce such beautiful works in art, music, and architecture and, on the other hand, soil the earth with blood and ashes to destroy one another. He studied the works of great composers and studied the political thoughts of the Greeks, the Romans, and the philosophers of the present time. A new political party was just starting to progress to fever in Germany while he was doing his college work. He'd read of another young man who loved architecture and art and had gotten involved with a revolutionary party in his home land. And that young man had become a convincing madman to a desperate people, who clung to his promises of their entitlement and superiority and then to his select few followers of elimination who followed his guidance toward the elimination of the innocent.

Another car thrashing through the leaves broke his thought. He and his grandmother, Mari, were the only members of the family that finally made it out alive after many heroic attempts by many fellow German-Catholics, Jews, and Austrians who gave their lives to save others. That's how they came to be in this place of Del Rey, Michigan. The neighborhood was comprised of Romanians from Austria who had escaped and settled to work in the car factories of Detroit. Many connections in Germany and the United States had ultimately brought them both to the right people at the right time. Certainly, his angel was watching out for him and his grandmother. Grandmother's young black and white cat walked by and caressed his leg with his tail while purring and circling around his feet.

"John, there's a phone call for you." Grandmother's voice slurred with her thick German accent just on the other side of the wall in the living room. Grandmother never referred to him as father. Their bonds were eternal, and he was still her little grandson.

He was made the assistant pastor at nearby St. John's Catholic Church when he graduated from seminary school. Prince, the cat, looked at him with bright green eyes. His grandmother had been the one who'd convinced the young father of the angel; so far through his journey there hadn't been much to show for. The father felt that he had not accomplished anything significant. Everything in his life, it seemed, had been lost; his father's face in the photo, his voice, and the way he sounded faded with the leaves. His mother's face so beautiful, so far away . . . He heard his grandmother again; he answered but didn't move.

The father's childhood accent had been quickly lost in the years that seemed like a lifetime ago. He was lucky. His angel, again, took care of everything. It was his angel who had convinced him to join the priesthood. Everything was all right.

"John?" his grandmother said softly.

"Coming, Grandmother," he answered.

He opened the screen door to a collection of homemade items embracing almost every square inch of her living room. The wonderful smell of fresh baked muffins was in the air. There were couch covers, light shade covers, covers for the pillows, covers for the picture frames, a cover for the radio in the corner, and there was even a crochet cover on the old, black phone. He smiled at his grandmother, and she returned the smile as she walked passed. Grandmother was glowing, as the sunshine kept her warm by the window. She was creating a blanket of maroon and blue, rocking back and forth as her needles pulled back and forth. Prince watched her hands busily moving.

Father John answered the phone. "Hello?"

"Good morning, Father John. How are you?" It was the monsignor.

"Good morning, monsignor." Father John carefully listened as he watched Grandmother's chair rocking back and forth. He listened awhile longer and asked, "New Mexico? Where is that?" Father John's mind quickly raced through the facts of his new assignment. The chair was rocking, the cat rubbing his head on Father John's pant leg. "I will have to take some time to coordinate Grandmother's trip to where again?"

"Yes, Santa Fe, New Mexico, Holy Faith."

Father John again listened, and a frown came over his face. He sat down and looked toward his grandmother. She was still involved with her project. He listened intently. As he hung up the phone, he sat in the chair. A look of dismay filled his young face. *Santa Fe, New Mexico—the city of holy faith—and I don't have any idea where it is. Well, well, Father Smitd, I guess I'd better find out.*

He looked at his clothing and started to wonder what people wore there. *What do I pack? What do I do with the cat?* The cat circled his leg and purred loudly; Father John scratched the cat's back. *Well, angel, I need your help again.* He stood up. Now he worried about what he would do about his aging grandmother. He had time to notice the clock in the hallway, which had a way of ticking time away whenever he had some hard decisions to make, was doing it again. He looked up at it. Prince was trying to get his attention for some reason.

"What's the matter?" Father John stroked the cat's soft black fur.

Grandmother always brushed Prince every night. The cat's fur was strikingly black, and the white part underneath was very clean. His nose was white with both cheeks black. His neck was white, and when he sat down, his white fur made a very distinct white "V". His front paws had short, white slippers, and his back ones had long, white socks. Prince was very disturbed, though, and in a verbal, unusual way. Father John got up from the chair and walked across the living room. He sat down in his chair and picked up the newspaper and gazed over at his grandmother Mari. She had fallen asleep, as she usually did. Her hands had stopped as if she had finished.

"Hey, Grandmother, that is a beautiful blanket! Look how beautiful" Father John would always make a big deal about everything she did for him.

She did not say a word.

Father John was thinking about his new assignment. Santa Fe, New Mexico. Way out west, in the middle of nowhere. The questions in his mind were coming at him so fast that he could not stop thinking. The clock in the hall kept on ticking louder and louder. Prince kept meowing, as if he wanted the young father's attention. Father John reached down to Prince and petted him and said, "Grandmother, what do you think is wrong with Prince?" Father John looked over to the window then to his grandmother.

She didn't move.

He looked at her. "Grandmother?" he asked. "Grandmother?" He walked over to her. He held her hand, and tears ran down his cheeks.

*   *   *

The funeral was well attended. John and Mari had no family members here in America, but the community supported Father John wholeheartedly. The funeral mass was attended by many members of the church. Father John, in the short time that he was at Holy Cross Church, had made many friends, including the mayor, the local unions, and the hospital staff that he frequently interacted with. That was Father John's style. His charisma and his love for others made him socially connected with everyone he came in contact with. He reached out to everyone with a smile and a handshake in order to meet strangers and quickly converted them to friends; he was truly a people person. The church delegation, the archbishop, and the monsignors were there to send Grandmother off. Father John Smitd was truly honored by the community.

After the arrangements, there was a week of meditation, and Father John looked toward the western sky—there beyond the horizon was his destiny. The day Father John was leaving, he went by the cemetery. He was tending to the grave with Prince in his arms. "Grandmother, I'm going now. I'm going now."

The bells of St. John's begun to toll, and the cat meowed good-bye. They both walked through the church garden and toward the railway station. He put Prince in the homemade carrying cage that he had made for him. Prince and he looked back at the graveyard one more time and walked away.

The Detroit archdiocese had made travel arrangements for Father John Smitd, and his paperwork was all in his hands. The young priest sat in the busy railway station, watching all the people going their own way. He took in the sounds of the steam engines building up their power to move down the line to their destinations, to carry their loads of cargo and people heading to all points. It all seemed disorganized and disarming to the father. His train was announced over the loudspeakers. He grabbed his large suitcase, his tow box, and the cage. Father John said comforting words to Prince as he boarded the Pullman carriage.

One of the baggage boys came about and tried to grab the cage from the father, and the father said, "No, this and this handbag stay with me."

The black boy did not say a word; he just looked inside the cage and smiled at the father and said, "It is a cat."

The father nodded yes. The father asked the boy if he could get him a small wooden box of some sort and made a gesture to indicate the size. The father was suddenly in a panic as to what to do with the cat's deposits on the train. He asked his angel to help him again—to come to the rescue. He stood between the train cars listening to the puffing of the engine and the wheels down below, and they started to turn and make noise as they hit the metal shanks on the timbers. The father was not sure that his request was going to be fulfilled. Then seconds later, up rushed the boy with a well-crafted box and some sawdust and sand inside. He smiled, "I have to get off the train now, Father; this should be good."

The father was surprised. "Tell me your name."

The baggage handler was trying say something and at the same time to jump off the train, and men from the station immediately started to grab the young baggage handler and beat him up.

The father yelled at them, "Stop! You! Stop! Stop, he' just a boy!"

The train moved faster away from the station. The father was paralyzed with fear and rage. His boyhood feelings immediately filled his body. The fight rolled off the train. The father started to jump off the train.

A large man grabbed the father and pulled him back on the train. He tried again to get off the train to assist the baggage boy, and the train conductor yelled at the father, "It's not your concern, Father!"

The father yelled back, "But the boy was helping me!"

The conductor pulled the father back onto the train. The father tried to fight the conductor, to no avail. The train started to pull away. "He was helping me. Leave him alone!"

This place could be as brutal as any place. All night he could not stop praying for the boy. The father filed a complaint with the conductor and with the train station and wanted some action. The father was cut in the forehead, and the conductor brought in some iodine and wrappings. The father refused. He would take care of it himself. He finally settled back into his sleeping quarters. After making sure that Prince got used to the surroundings, he began writing in his journal. He cried.

The father made several attempts to get information about what had happened. The train conductor made gestures to the father, indicating that he would get back to the father and find out what had happened. The father was sure, given the conductor's attitude, that nothing was going to be investigated. Prince slept at his side that night.

Father John woke up in the early morning to the sound of the moving train. He said his prayers then fed Prince and proceeded to look over the many notes about the Catholic efforts in the areas of the Southwest. There were many gaps in the history books, and the father was going to have to get that information somehow. He had spent a few evenings scrounging through the limited library back at the seminary school. There were many questions about his new assignment in Santa Fe, New Mexico.

The train began the journey south then east through the plush wetlands and the great planting fields of mid-America. He was amazed at the size of the great rivers the train had crossed. His journey began in spring. At every stop, he met the most interesting people along the way—farmers; ranchers from Ohio; statesmen from Indiana and Illinois; families from Kansas, Missouri, Nebraska, or Iowa; lawmen from Oklahoma; cattlemen from Texas; trappers from Colorado, rich people, and poor people. And the father was eager to talk to as many as he could; that was his nature. All of them were following a dream of some sort—a dream of creating something for themselves, if not for their families. Some of the characters he talked to were certainly out for themselves, like a couple of hombres—that's what they called themselves—who said they were in "banking." These "hombres" needed to be blessed, they said. So the father blessed them. Not a full blessing, you understand, because the father knew well enough that these hombres were not on the level.

The trip was long and cold at night and not very comfortable. The train would have to stop and pick up coal, and the conductors and the engineers would have discussions with natives on the way, which confused the father. Why were they called "Indians" when they were not from India? That was very strange. At the stops, he would pull out Prince, and the other passengers would marvel at the cat, as if it was the strangest zoo animal in the world. They would have the greatest range of reactions—from fear to great curiosity—that the father had ever seen. Prince took all in stride like felines always do; he just ignored everyone. A cat on a train was an oddity.

The father and Prince enjoyed looking out the carriage window at the endless vistas of the plains. The father just kept on thinking about his new assignment and missing his grandmother. He just couldn't imagine what it was going to be like. The archbishop in Detroit had given him a map;

he started to unfold it. He was trying to follow what he thought was the Santa Fe Trail. His finger traced the faded line where one night, he traced the journey by candlelight. His concentration was interrupted by a raspy voice on the other side of the map.

"Now, at first glance, I thought you had a skunk with you, Padre?"

The father put the map down. "Oh my cat. No, that is Prince; he is my cat."

"Oh, may I have seat?" The stranger stopped and sat downs opposite the father as the train rumbled along as usual.

The father asked, "Padre?"

The stranger stretched out his hand. "My name is Earl Stives, Padre, and *padre* out here in the West is Spanish for *father!*"

"Oh," said Father John. "I'm Padre John Smitd."

"Is it dangerous?"

"Oh no," said the father. "He's pretty tame. However, he will scratch you if he does get upset."

Earl just sat there staring at Prince. Prince just stared right back. "Is he upset at me right now?" Earl asked.

The father leans forward and looked into Prince's eyes, which were still fixed on Earl. "I think he just doesn't know you."

"Well, I'll just warm up to him slowly then," said Earl. "So where, are you headed, Padre?"

"To a place called Santa Fe," the father explained.

"Really," said Earl.

"Do you know this place?" asked the father.

"Yes, sir, Padre; I know the area pretty well."

"What happened to your head?" asked Earl.

The father started to tell the story, and Earl interrupted him. "Padre, you don't have to tell me. I saw it all. And if you don't mind, I'll go ahead and take care of things for you back there. You see, I'm an attorney; I have already taken down some information on the incident at the station. I have spent the last day or so recording the facts and following up with the conductor. My office in Washington will contact me and will get something done about the matter."

Father John was elated. "Will you? Thank you. Will you find out for me who that boy was, please?" he asked.

"Don't worry," said Earl as made himself more comfortable.

The father was at ease about what his new friend was going to do for him, and Prince was doing fine with Earl too. Earl put his carrying case on the top rack and cleared out an area for himself. He started to talk to Prince, and the cat jumped over to his seat, which surprised the father. Prince sat there and looked at Earl. Earl pulled some dried meat and gave it to Prince, and the cat sniffed at it and ate some of it.

"I think we're going to be friends, Father. Yeah, anything you want to know about the Southwest or Santa Fe, you just ask. I love to talk; that's why I'm a lawyer. I love to talk."

So Father John said, "Tell me about the history of the Southwest. I couldn't find many books in the seminary to get me prepared for my assignment in Santa Fe."

Earl started by telling the father about the native population and how the ancient ones had settled there in the four corners area. They built beautiful cities out of rock and wood in a place called Chaco Canyon. "They said their roads were paved with stone!" Earl kept on telling his story into the day as the train kept on traveling through the countryside. The roads led up to the mountains of Colorado. This civilization lasted until a great drought made it necessary for them to find other water sources and they had to leave for the great river, which ran down from the great, white, snow-covered mountains. This split up the great population into many pueblos. They were all a peaceful people, who mostly planted corn and beans and kept to themselves. They made beautiful pottery and blankets for hundreds of years, and all the people were successful trading amongst themselves.

Father John loved the tutorial and kept notes.

But who was this man? Was he a hombre like those other two he had met or what? Days and nights kept on rumbling by. Prince, the father, and Earl were enjoying the trip. Father John stopped Earl to offer him food he had packed during one of the stops in a little town somewhere in Kansas; it seemed like yesterday that he had left Detroit. Earl, in kind, offered the father some of his food. The both looked at each other's offering. Earl looked at the father's portion, which was a meat product from Germany and a slice of tomato on top. Earl was not used to raw meat. The father took a piece of dried meat and started to chew on it. He commented that it was certainly salty.

Earl said, "I think we need to burn this baby!" as he chewed on his portion.

They both laughed, while learning about each other's ways. The father was curious as to how Earl knew so much about the Native Americans, Mexicans, Spanish, and the Southwest. Earl explained that his older brother had been a trapper out there in the Santa Fe/Taos area and had written to him so many times about the people that Earl had a great understanding about the area; also, Earl had been there many times before.

Father John was so grateful that his angel had led this man to him. It was like having a great book on the train with him. "So, Earl, where are you headed? May I ask?"

"Well, Padre," Earl said while he looked at the cat. "It looks like I'm making friends with Prince here. I was going to Taos, but I've change my mind in the last two days. I'm going to Santa Fe. I have some business to take care of."

The father just looked Earl. Earl was a well-dressed man with good manners about him, and the father felt comfortable with him. Prince, on the other hand, was, as usual, making up his own mind. The cat just sat there, staring at Earl.

The father asked Earl to share more about Santa Fe later. The father was tired; he needed some rest. He was going to take a nap. Prince jumped back to the father's side to watch over him and stare at Earl, and Earl stared back. The sun set with brilliant reds, purples, pinks, and blues and a spectacular vision to the west came into view. The father wasn't really sure, but it seemed there was snow capped mountains in the distance. It must be the light of the sunset or his eyes were getting tired. The train was slowing down. They were stopping for the night. He would ask Earl in the morning. Father and Prince retired to their cabin.

The morning sunshine was barely making an announcement in the east when Prince was at father's side wanting his morning greeting. At five—thirty every morning, Prince would wake father for Morning Prayer. The father would go through his usual rosary and meditation. Prince would observe and stand guard. This morning was no exception.

At about seven, Earl knocked at the door. "You up, Father?" I know this great place to get a great breakfast!"

The father said, "I'll meet you outside in just a minute." He prepared Prince and left him there. "Now I'll leave you some food, and there's your box. I'll be back." He grabbed his new blazer that Earl had given him; it was a leather blazer. He had never seen anything like this before this in his life. He was surprised at what he looked like. He had seen the old western movie before, and he thought he would try it on for size. He walked out the corridor and out the railcar, and there stood Earl smiling. "My, don't you look the sight."

They ate breakfast in an old café in Raton, New Mexico. The folks inside were gracious and friendly to Earl, and everyone knew him. Father John was astonished at his popularity but did not say a word. Earl carried on conversations about cattle and ranching with the locals as if he was connected somehow. Earl introduced almost everyone in the café to the father. It was very impressive.

Then it was time to get on back on the train and head south. The father asked Earl about the mountains and the snow, and Earl confirmed that the father had seen snow that was left over from last winter; it stayed up there until June sometimes. The father was spellbound.

Father John took out the crafted wood box with fine cedar chips and Prince would go to the box, relieve himself, and stare at Earl. Earl was amazed the animal was trained to do that stuff. The cat was through and covered his business and came on back and sat there near the father and looked out the window. The father would have his morning routines, and the cat would follow him back and forth; wherever the father went, that's where the cat went. Others on the train just made room for the cat and the padre. The train stopped and pick up or dropped off more riders along the way, the scenery change a bit, and the riders change; fewer and fewer cars were to be seen at each stop. The further south the train went, the more livestock and the more horses came into view; the father was not used to seeing that many horses or cows all at once. He would ask Earl about everything and write everything down in his little notebook. Earl loved to tell stories about whatever questions the father had.

"Earl, the names are predominantly Spanish all over this area?" asked the Father.

Earl elaborated on the first Europeans on the continent, who were from Spain. Although Columbus was Italian, it was the king and queen of Spain who financed the expeditions into the new world. Some expeditions went into Louisiana and into Mexico from Florida and Cuba. The Spanish moved up the Rio Grande and discovered the Acoma Pueblo, where all the buildings were whitewashed at the time, and in the sunset, they looked like gold, so one monk and a Moorish black man, a soldier from Africa, sent back word of some cities of gold. Then Spain sent expeditions led by a man named Coronado. Coronado and his men came through New Mexico, Oklahoma, Arizona, and all over, looking for God, glory, and gold, but didn't find any. So he went back to Spain to report his findings to the royalty. The King and Queen of Spain sent back people to settle the land for Spain. This all happened in the latter part of the 1500s. In the land where the natives had no concept of property or government, a European way of life had its consequences for the native population.

Another conquistador named Oñate came through the area and almost wiped out the native population by being a tyrant and a bully. The natives tolerated it for about one hundred years, until about 1680; then the pueblo natives revolted against the Spanish and drove all the Spanish settlers back down to El Paso. The natives were victorious over the Spanish, but their problems only started. The natives had considered themselves an oppressed society under Spanish rule. Their victory turned to an even worse situation with the Navajo, Apache and Ute tribes left unchecked.

The Spanish had taken over their land and, yes, had given them last names that were Spanish and yes had given them religion, but they had also given them protection from renegade tribes of Navajo, Apache and the Utes, who started to steal everything that was not tied down. That was what they had forgotten after all these years, and things got a little bit nasty here. Once the Spanish soldiers, with their armor, rifles, and horses, which appeared to be like spirits of fire galloping across the plains, were no longer around to protect the pueblos, the free riders from the north, south and east were free to come right in and take advantage of all the people. Women were stolen, artifacts were stolen, and the pueblo culture was ransacked.

Meanwhile, in Spain, Queen Isabella and King Ferdinand did not like the idea of their subjects being chased out of their own land; that was not acceptable. It took a year and half to organize their response. The Royals employed a young man named Don Diego de Vargas and his company of men to go back to Santa Fe. By the time he arrived with his men, the natives were glad to see the Spanish again. Men and women with carts full of house wares started to move up the Rio Grande with last names such as Ortiz, Rodriguez, C de Baca, Salas, Perez, Valdez, Trujillo, Sandoval, Chavez, Martinez, Roybal, Sanchez, Quintana, Romero, Aragon, Dominguez, Fernandez, Garcia, Herrera, Lopez, Valdez, Urioste, Rios, Valdez, Zamora, Portillo, and Maes (the list was so long it took up a whole page)—a year had passed. Don Diego and his men marched in and set up a government that was somewhat decent. Oh, there were little fights here and there, during which native people were killed, but all in all, it was a peaceful takeover. Santa Feans celebrate the takeover with La Fiesta every year. The Spanish peoples came back in, the pueblos were protected again, the Navajos, the Apaches and the Utes started to behave again, and so began the multicultural world of the Southwest as it exists today.

Father John was taking notes as fast as he could. Prince was getting closer to Earl. Earl was getting very curious as to what the cat was up to. Earl said, "What do you suppose he's up to?"

"He's just trying to figure you out," said father John.

Prince sat near Earl and stared with those big green eyes at him. Earl continued. Prince tried to smell his coat, and Earl let him, with caution of course. "These Indians—"

"Stop!" Father John interrupted. "They're not from India, correct?"

"But that's what they are called; I know, silly, isn't it?" Earl replied.

Father John shook his head.

"Are you going to let me tell the story or not?"

"Okay, then," the father said.

"Okay," Earl said, "okay."

Spain had too many problems in the new world. New Mexico was too far away, and it conceded its control of the territory to Mexico, which really did not go well with the Spanish subjects who had already been in New Mexico for more than one hundred years. Mexico immediately took control, and that wasn't really a good thing for any of the parties concerned. The Spanish families resented Mexican rule The Native Americans didn't care for their type of government, and the United States of America really didn't like the idea of Mexico encroaching into U.S. land. "But you know who really got mad, padre?"

Father looked at Earl as he rocked back and forth in his seat.

"The Texans." They wanted New Mexico for themselves—at least half of it anyways. They saw that, if they could fight to increase their line all the way to the Rio Grande, they could get Santa Fe, Taos, and some of the Rocky Mountains. That was their plan and created the maps to increase their territory. "I'm kind of taking liberty with the history a bit, but that's how it played out."

"So I should be wary of Texans, then," said the father."

"No, just kidding, Father," said Earl,

The father took more notes.

Father John, Earl, and Prince rode the train along the Rockies. Earl continued, "The Americans weren't all that honorable either, I could tell you a story or two about Kit Carson and his crew."

The father wrote as much as you could and looked out the window at the wonderful scenery as the train made its echoing sounds through the canyons and Prince explored every chance he could through the cabins. His master was not far away to stop his exploration.

As the train headed south, the conversations between Earl and the father seemed endless; the train continued cutting through the beautiful vistas stopping at each loading station to load passengers or have material loaded or unloaded, there was a coordinated dance about the whole procedure. The train pulled away from each stop, the Father. Earl, and Prince looked at the beautiful views of northern New Mexico and the new faces on the car and laughed together, talked, read books, and spent time together all the way to their last stop of the journey. The train chugged through the last canyons and broke through a wonderful vision of the Ortiz Mountains, the sight of active gold mines, according to Earl. The train struggled to a stop at the station in Lamy, New Mexico.

Father snapped his fingers for Prince to get in his carrier, and like a trooper, the cat strolled right in. Earl again was amazed. The father was in amazement at the mountains—their size, their magnitude, and their beauty. "This place is so beautiful, Earl!"

Earl turned around and said, "This *is* God's country, Padre!"

Father eyes were just filled in wonder. His thoughts were of his grandmother Mari. She would have loved it here. This place seemed like a world away from his childhood; his pictures of torment, his books and his history were being unloaded from the train. His thoughts were interrupted by a car racing down the dirt road, its dusty trail rising. The father was not used to seeing such a sight. It was like an old silent movie with a piano in the background. There was a flatbed truck giving chase to the car, both keeping pace and heading right towards the train station.

The car came to a dusty halt by the train parking area, and the driver door opened. A tall man opened the door and he emerged from the car, his black—and red-trimmed robe, falling to his feet, fluttered in the dust and breeze. The man was obviously a monsignor who walked towards the platform. He motioned over to the father and greeted him with a hard handshake. "Good morning, Father Smith. I'm Monsignor Henry Dimor. Welcome to Santa Fe. How was your trip?"

Father John replied, "Father Smitd, S-M-I-T-D."

"Oh, I'm sorry. Your papers are all under Smith. We'll have to address that later. In the meantime, let's get your things, and get into town." The monsignor noticed the carrier the father was holding. "What is that, may I ask?"

Father John's awe at the beauty around him and the joy of being here were quickly diminishing.

Earl's voice loomed from behind. "That's mine. It's a rare cat."

Father John started to speak, but before he could, Monsignor Dimor, shouted, "Good. There are to be no animals in the rectory!"

Father John's heart sank.

Earl greeted the monsignor. "I'm Earl Stives."

"I know you, but from where?" said the monsignor.

"I'm a legal council from the East, your grace," said Earl. The monsignor did not take Earl's hand. "The father was helping me out," continued Earl.

"Excuse me, monsignor," Father John interrupted. "Mr. Stives has been very helpful to me as well. He has provided me background information about the Southwest and Santa Fe as well, and we have become good friends on the journey here."

"Excuse my manners, Mr. Stives. Nice to meet you. Can we offer you a ride into Santa Fe?" The monsignor smiled halfway. "We can have your baggage brought in as well, Mr. Stives."

"Thank you," said Earl.

They all climbed into the black 1935 Chevy, the monsignor in the driver's seat. In the front passenger's seat, a priest sat writing furiously on a tablet while two men loaded up their belongings into a truck behind the car. The monsignor asked Earl about the carrier with Prince inside, and Earl insisted that the cat had to be handheld, that it was like family to him. The monsignor gave him a blank look.

The monsignor introduced, "Oh, by the way, Father Smith, Mr. Steward, this is Father Mar'niez" Both father John and Earl corrected their names to Father Martinez and so did Father Martinez in the way the monsignor pronounced his last name. It was Martinez not Mar'iez

The ride into Santa Fe was about forty-five minutes from Lamy. Father John was amazed as the vistas passed by. The monsignor drove unusually fast on the dirt road, and Father Martinez's head rocked back and forth as he wrote on his tablet. "I normally let Father Juan drive, but he drives too slowly," said the monsignor.

Father Martinez shook his said.

As they neared Santa Fe, Father John noticed buildings that seemed to blend into the landscape as if they belonged. He asked what type of construction these buildings were.

The monsignor answered, "Primitive."

Father Martinez shook his head in the front seat and continued to write in his tablet.

Earl said, "I'll explain it to you later, Padre."

Father John checked with Prince, and the cat was just fine in his carrier. The father looked at Earl, and Earl winked and nodded. Father John took comfort in knowing that Earl was going to take responsibility for Prince given this unforeseen complication. Thank God that Prince had gotten used to Earl these days on the train. He would have to have some sort of arrangement with the monsignor to get his grandmother's cat back. But how? How bad was this?

The dirt road wound its way through the large foothills, and across the way were large mountains to the west. Earl called them the Jemez Mountains, he said that within those mountains near the Puye Cliffs, lay a secret-which Earl could tell the father about one day. The monsignor dismissed the whole thing as hogwash. Earl winked at Father Juan again. Father John was not sure about this winking business and was sure to ask Earl about it later.

Soon they came over the rise to see the valley, and Father John caught the first view of Santa Fe; it was a vision of peace. The town seemed to be caressed by the mountains, the richness of its center manifested by small-needled pine trees and then tall cottonwood trees. Buildings were nestled in with careful harmony and the distinct browns and greens of the landscape. The brightest blue sky that stretched out endlessly; the father sat there mesmerized. Father John felt is if he had come home. He felt like he was alone in that car. He felt like he had a mission to fulfill here in Santa Fe. A chill filled his whole body. Father John started to smile. He heard his grandmother's voice, her deep German accent, *"John, this is good."* Father John did not know what she meant, but he never questioned grandmother's directives. He guessed she had assumed the position of his angel now. The largest building Father John could see was the cathedral. It was hewn of stone, and it looked out of place for some reason. It faced west with gothic nobility in the middle of a tranquil, serene landscape.

The road followed the old Santa Fe Trail, according to Earl, as they neared the city; they came in on College Street. Father John was amazed at the construction of the houses. Earl said, "Remember we discussed the use of earth and mud products for the construction of houses; well those are adobe structures made of mud bricks. They're made of a certain type of clay mud, sand, and straw, dried in the sun; and they make a pretty darn good house. Oh, sorry about that, your highness."

The monsignor just drove and did not comment. Father Martinez looked back at Earl and smiled. Earl winked at him.

They passed St. Michael's College and the high school; Loretto's School for Girls; and a small, gothic structure, the Loretto Chapel.

Father Martinez said, "The chapel houses a staircase that was built without any nails by some unknown carpenter who drifted into town then drifted away after completing the work.

Earl said, "Well, that's quite a miracle, isn't?"

Nobody took the bait.

"Clergy have no sense of humor," Earl said.

Father John replied, "I got it."

The car made its way toward the cathedral's walled entry, which was paved with brick, the driveway winding toward the rectory. The scene inside the walls was quite different from that of the town outside. Lilac bushes, plush grass, fruit trees, and large pine trees created a beautiful haven retreat from the world outside. Father John couldn't help to think that the small world in here was a replica of Paris or someplace in Europe somewhere. They all disembarked, unloaded, and Father John was shown his quarters by some ladies and men, who quickly unloaded the vehicles. Earl was assisted with his belongings by the two men in the truck and they discussed the maneuvers in Spanish as if he had known them forever with pats on theirs backs. They all pointed towards the La Fonda Hotel. The monsignor looked on with disdain as he walked in towards the rectory.

While all this was going on, Father John kept an eye on Prince's carrier, and Earl winked at him. "Father John, let's get together for dinner tonight; we'll discuss the trip. Okay?" Earl yelled out as he put the Prince's carrier in the car.

Father John responded, "That would be good!"

The car and the truck pulled out of the driveway making their way into the street.

LA FONDA GIL SANCHEZ 08
HOTEL

The father was exhausted from all the excitement. His new surroundings were too much to take in at once. The staff led him towards his accommodations through narrow hallways and low doorways. They opened the door to his room. He looked around at the earth walls of his room and it felt so comfortable that the surroundings touched his soul and he felt safe. It was odd. The walls were thick, around a foot or so. The rooms were cool and yet warm. The ceilings were made out of round beams and, between them, cedar strips that gave off a wonderful aroma; it made you relax naturally. The walls were immaculately white; the floors were wooden and beautifully polished to a mirror finish. Some of the statutes and crosses were not familiar; some seemed homemade. Father John needed to get with Father Martinez, there is always that moment in ones' life when you're away in a strange place, there is an emptiness that fills you. And even though the young priest was trained that he was not alone, he felt alone. For some reason he knew that Father Martinez was thinking about him.

Father Martinez rushed in, startling Father John. "Father Martinez, I was just thinking about you."

"I know." Father Martinez quickly laid some towels on the small bed. "The monsignor is a man who is kind of . . ." Father Martinez's accent was now very clear. Father John tried to figure out what he was trying to say. "Como se dice, difficult."

Father John just smiled. "Oh I figured that out when he opened his mouth."

They both sat down and laughed. They talked. Father Martinez's first name was Juan, same as father John, except the former had two other names, which was typical for Hispanics in the area. He was Juan Miguel Jesus Martinez. The family of Juan Miguel Jesus Martinez had come over with Don Diego de Vargas. He was very proud of his heritage and the culture. He was going to be a wonderful source of knowledge for father John. His family was from Taos, New Mexico. They sat and talked for an hour and introduced themselves. They were getting to know each other—as if they were brothers who had parted ways a long time ago and had long found immediate strength in each other; a sense of blessing was placed upon them. They both agreed that something had happened—that for some reason they were both on a new adventure. And while neither knew what that adventure was, they felt good about their alliance.

"I have a confession to make, though," Father John said.

"Already?" Father Juan answered.

"The cat is mine."

"I know," Father Juan said.

They both laughed.

"How do you know that?" Father John asked.

Father Juan replied, "I saw your reaction when the Monsignor stated there were to be no cats in the rectory at the station!"

"So what can I do?" Father John asked.

"Nothing now," Father Juan told him. "We'll figure something out."

"Would you join me for dinner tonight and meet my friend?" Father John asked.

The fathers left the rectory and went out through the beautiful grounds and into the evening toward San Francisco Street and La Fonda Hotel to meet with Earl. The hotel was pueblo style, and natives sold their wares, which were amazing to Father John, around the side of the building. Father John stopped to handle the jewelry with care and ask questions about how it was made, what material it was made of, and what tribe the sellers were from.

Father Juan smiled, enjoying watching the excitement of a person who was appreciating the wonderment of one of the cultures that was Santa Fe. "You'll have time to learn all there is to learn about all this while you are here." Father Juan puts his arm around Father John's neck as they walked though the doorway.

Father John heard the sound of a train whistle. "I didn't know the train came into town?" he asked.

Father Juan explained that the train in town was the Chili Line; it served northern New Mexico, bringing in loads of lumber, glass for windows, lamps, tables, chairs and other furniture from the Eastern seaboard to the area from the Lamy Railroad Station.

The fathers asked the desk clerk for Earl's room number, and they were surprised when they learned the number; his room was on the top floor of three-story building. The hotel was beautifully decorated. As the fathers entered the double doors, they noticed there were people everywhere, in every hallway. Father John noticed the polished flagstone shaped floors, curios on every shelf to be sold filled the hallways and paintings lined the walls. The finest china in the dining rooms, drapery from the East and you could tell there were very rich people around. The fathers made their way toward the fancy elevator. Some politicians stood at the end of the great hallway, three of whom made sure they greeted the fathers with smiles that stretched from here to the other side of Santa Fe.

"Fathers, we are so glad to see you again!"

How are you?" two of the politicians chimed, each shaking the fathers' hands so aggressively their arms almost came out of the sockets.

Father Juan said, "You've never met us before."

The other politician replied, "That's right. We are here to meet at state legislature, and we love Santa Fe."

"Santa Fe is beautiful," Father John agreed.

"You all have good day!" the politicians said as they all rushed off.

Both fathers got in the elevator and Father Juan pushed the number three button.

Father Juan looked at Father John. "You have to learn to become a good politician to survive in this archdiocese," he said. "Y'all have a good day!" And they both laughed as the elevator ascended.

They walked down the beautifully decorated corridor and knocked on the door. Earl opened it. The father's eyes were captivated by what they were looking at; it was the best hotel room he had ever seen. It was huge.

"Come in, Padres!" Earl was in a white smoking jacket, smoking his cigar. The room was decorated in lavish velvet material, and the whole place was spotless and fit for a king. The fathers walked in slowly with mouths opened and inspected everything.

"Well, Earl, this is amazing!" Father Juan said.

"Not bad," said Earl.

They went through the room and outside through the double doors to the patio and gazed out at the town, and there was the cathedral and the rest of Santa Fe caressed by the Sangre de Cristo Mountains. The air was crisp and clean. The smell of piñon wood tinted the air. The mountains had a golden stain on them as the sun set to the west.

"You fathers want dinner here in the room or downstairs in the dining hall?" asked Earl.

"It doesn't matter to us, Earl," said Father John. "Earl, where is Prince?"

Earl led Father John to another bedroom. He opened the door, and there on the bed was Prince, very content with his tail moving as if he was the king of his room. He immediately meowed to his master. Father John explained the situations to Prince, and Prince just rubbed against him and meowed and took it all in. Father Johns inspected the room and the cat's box. The room was better than the one in which the father was staying in. That was okay, as long as Prince was being cared for.

They all went downstairs for dinner. The hotel was still busy and full of all kinds of people. Earl Stives had changed from his casual dress to a nice suit. Father John was especially impressed with how professional Earl looked. "You look very nice Earl." Said Father John,

"Thank you, Padre. This is what I look like when I appear in court—a blue suit, a white shirt, and a red tie; the first impression is the most important, Father; never forget that."

Earl tipped the woman at the door, and the trio got the best table. All the tables were full, the table they got was right next to some important-looking men at a table; Earl tipped his hat to the gentlemen as they all sat down.

Father Juan said to Earl, "It's not often I get to sit near the mayor at dinner."

"It's about time you sit by him, don't you think?" asked Earl.

Father Juan nodded. There were drinks sent to them all during dinner that night, and Father John was getting the feeling that Earl was more important than he was leading them to believe. "All right now; what's going on, Earl? Who are you?" Father John inquired.

"Father it's all a matter of perception," Earl whispered. "That's what lawyers are all about. They paint a picture, a perception, and tie it all together with words that no one understands. They present it in a court of law and, poof, it's done—a man, or law, or perception is changed forever, for the good of society or bad." Earl settled back in his chair and lit his cigar.

Father Juan asks, "Which side do you represent, Señor Earl?"

Earl stared at his plate—the remains of choice beef steak, chili, potatoes, and tortillas—and glass—the best tequila in town. Earl started to laugh, "Ah, Father Juan, you are sharp. You don't let a statement go, do you? Okay, I'll answer that.

"I used to think that everything I did was honorable, but then when you scratch the surface, you began to realize that the bigger the task, the bigger the money, the less the honor there was in it. The higher the stakes and the higher the profiles of the men I got involved with, the worse the situations would get. The West was wide open for corruption; banks, railroad, and land was all set up for the taking. Taking advantage of the people in the West was in style for a while, until some us began to think about the consequences.

"My brother, Sam, kept me informed about some of the interactions between the old Spanish land grant holders and the fancy lawyers that came in and set up some quit-claim deeds, moving old reservation lines and destroying old railroad papers and I started to fight some of the changes in Washington, to protect New Mexico from becoming a wasteland. So I guess, I was on the bad side at one time, and now I have seen the light."

Father John smiled at Earl. "There is much more to learn about you, isn't there?"

The dinner ended, and they all parted at the end of the big hall.

"Don't worry about Prince," called Earl. "He'll have his own maid assigned to him."

Father John waved back.

Father John and Father Juan strolled through the plaza, passing old-style lantern lights and, in the middle, a stone monument dedicated to people who struggled to get to Santa Fe at the end of the Santa Fe Trail. Men and some women were sitting in the plaza—that is what father Juan called it. In the north side was the Palace of the Governors, which had a long portal; again the architecture was adobe, very earthy, and Father John loved it. They made their way back to the rectory near the cathedral. The rectory was made out of adobe; it was earthy and warm at the end of the long hallway.

On Father John's first night in Santa Fe, the night was chilled with crisp, cooled, pined, air by the piñon wood fires in the distance. He said his prayers until midnight then stepped outside to view the most magnificent sky full of stars he had ever seen. He had forgotten that Santa Fe was at seven thousand feet above sea level. He stared at the heavens above. He located the North Star and could not believe his eyes; so many stars were visible here at night. He felt he was very close to God at this moment. He got on his knees. He made the sign of the cross. The women that worked in the rectory made sure that the father's room was well supplied with blankets, but there in the corner of the room hanging on a chair was the blanket that his grandmother had made him. He could hear the Chili Line's whistle in the distance as he fell asleep in the warmth of his bed.

Over the next few days, Father John and Father Juan worked closely together in the rectory's office, taking care of the monsignor's busy work—the administrative work for the archdiocese, the daily masses, and the mission work—and preparing to put up with monsignor's attitude toward everything. It was negative, to say the least. The father came to find out that the monsignor's and the archbishop's attitudes didn't fit here; Father John felt that they both were mad at something and couldn't quite figure it out. Father John would try to get some conversations going with the monsignor at certain times, but it was like trying to trap a wild animal. Father John's attempts were failing at every juncture.

"Monsignor." Father John greeted.

"Yes," said the monsignor.

"Monsignor, where are you from?" would asked Father John.

"Don't you have anything to do?" would respond the monsignor.

Father John responded, "Well, yes I do." "Well you'd better get to it, then!" the monsignor would respond as he walked away.

"Your name will never be changed," said Father Juan.

"Why?" Father John responded.

Father Juan said, "Because that's the way he is. Your last name is now Smith. Face it."

Father John walked into the main hallway of the rectory office. The monsignor was talking to some men from city hall. Father John walked over to the monsignor. "Monsignor, about my paperwork for the name change?"

Monsignor Dimor did not respond to Father John's question. Instead, he said, "Father John, I would like you to meet some of the mayor's staff. They are here to discuss some of the new additions to the school on College Street that you are going to be involved with."

The introductions went on, and the meeting commenced. Father John never got an answer that day. The next day however, the monsignor did apologize for his abrupt behavior, saying he would get back to the name change. That's how things went on at the office—no plans just reactions to whatever the monsignor had going on. And the fathers had to immediately react to his lack of organization. Father John truly did not like this at all. Father Juan had been here all this time, years, being mistreated, taking all this abuse; all things had to stop for this monsignor, and the father just adapted. But Father John was not willing to adapt, however right or wrong. People shouldn't be treated in that manner. Father John was taken back to his memories of childhood and he did not like the feeling. Prince had already accepted Father Juan and showed love and acceptance, Prince was a prince; the monsignor was a man that set up walls that were hard to bring down, it was hard for the father to compare a human and an animal.

Father Juan and Earl came in from the Plaza and brought in some food for all. "What you thinking about father?" asked Father Juan. Father John didn't answer. He just got up and they all decided to go to Earl's big hotel room and enjoyed the afternoon.

*   *   *

One day, Father John and Father Juan were in the office with the monsignor. "Monsignor, I would like to talk to you about organizing your time, and our time, both father Juan's and mine."

Father Juan, who had just taken a bite of an apple, sat there with his mouth open.

"What exactly do you mean, Father John?" the monsignor finally replied.

Father John proceeded carefully. "I mean both of us"—Father Juan rolled his eyes—"both of us need to be able to organize our time and we feel that we cannot, because we are just reacting to your schedule all the time."

The room was very quiet. The clock on the wall was the only sound you could hear. Father Juan started to sweat. He could not swallow. The monsignor started to chew on his lip. This was bad. Father Juan knew this. He looked at Father John. Father John looked straight at the monsignor, knowing that Father Juan was looking at him. It seemed like nothing was going on; time was standing still. The monsignor finally stood up. The fathers looked up; the room seemed to shrink. The monsignor spoke. "Well I guess I should share my schedule with you both. I will consider that in the future." Monsignor Dimor walked out in a hurry.

Father Juan finally swallowed. "Are you out of your mind?"

"What?" Father John smiled.

Father Juan continued, "You are purposely challenging him!" He pointed as he said this.

Father John said, "Look, he has to know that we are not his puppets."

Father Juan replied, "We are his puppets!"

"He will respect me for this," Father John declared.

Father Juan retorted, "He will transfer you for this!"

Weeks went on. No transfers came to fruition and no schedules were handed down; life was pretty hectic for the fathers. Father John would go over and see Prince in his hotel suite and he, Earl, and the cat would spend quality time together. Earl would update him on what was going on in the communities in New Mexico. Each evening, the two would sit and talk, discussing the acequias, the Rio Grande, the local politics, and the advancement of a man named Hitler in Europe. Father Juan would join in sometimes, and the trio became great friends; they would enjoy playing cards and watching the sunsets from the patio. Prince would sit and watch them and wag his tail with approval. Father John noticed that Prince was getting bigger and closer to Earl and that the two had a good relationship, which was good. Earl called him Dude sometimes, but Prince always came to Father John whenever he was around.

Father John began to learn more about *la gente*, the people, around Santa Fe. Each barrio, or neighborhood, had its own particular group of people with a sense of pride and belonging. The south side had its church on

Agua Fria, San Isidro had their church further west, St. Anne's Church was up further towards the middle of town and the Guadalupe Church was where the train ran right in front of it; everywhere in Santa Fe there was either a monument or a church that signified the people's pride in their own particular barrio.

Archbishop Lamy who had built the cathedral had a great significance to Santa Fe; it depended on who you talked to. If you talked to Father Juan, it was negative based on the historical implications, and if you talked to the monsignor, he was the greatest archbishop of all time; Father John was determined to get the stories straight. The city was busy with car dealers, dress shops, drugstores and curio shops in and around the plaza fanned out toward the river. A few barbershops lined the avenue near the railroad station. The restaurants downtown were good, and hotels were a nice place for visitors to hang their hats. Cars were everywhere in the streets, but men on horseback still crossed through town every once and awhile dressed in the traditional dress of the cowboy. Trucks with haystacks in the back were a common sight, as were cows being towed along the tree-lined streets in trailers behind trucks. Everyone took the time to talk to each other, sometimes in Spanish and sometimes in English. The problem was you never knew what language was coming at you; you just had to be prepared. Father Juan spent time coaching Father John, giving him Spanish lessons into the night. "Pero you say it peeeerrrro, gato, now you, gaaaatoooo."

Father Juan and Father John traveled to the native pueblos together to do mission work along with the Franciscan fathers. They were the original sect that had come here with the explorers from Spain. They would get invited to the ceremonies and the meals. The tradition was that you were only invited to a pueblo once; once you'd accepted the initial invitation, you were expected to be there from then on. The next time you came you had to bring something, and on your third visit, you had to bring something to cook. Another tradition of the great pueblos of northern New Mexico that Father John quickly learned was that you never clapped at their ceremonies. Doing so would be just like clapping at Mass; it wasn't done.

The families of the pueblos were friendly and eager to share their time with the fathers. After one such trip, during which Father John got to meet all of Father Juan's family in Taos, they were traveling back through the big canyon on the Rio Grande in the Chevy. Father John asked Father Juan about Archbishop Lamy.

Father Juan explained that this archbishop had been sent to Santa Fe as an assignment from France, and when he'd arrived here in the later part of the 1800's, the cathedral had been called La Parroquia and had served the community. It was a large structure made of adobe. The archbishop did not like the building at all, and he had it thrown down for the exemption of a small portion of it to serve mass. He had seen fit to bring in some Italian stonemasons and built a gothic structure to resemble the churches he was used to in France. The archbishop arranged for laborers get the huge stones from Galisteo area to build the new cathedral. The current cathedral was completed in 1884 long after the after the archbishop had died, but the steeples were never completed, workmen were always getting hurt in the process.

In the meantime, Archbishop Lamy alienated everyone he came in contact with, including Father Juan's great-grandfather from Taos. Archbishop Lamy considered the Spanish, the Mexicans, and the Native Americans as primitives and did not like being here. For long period of time, all the Catholics here were cut off from Durango, Mexico in the 16th Century through the time he arrived the population here in New Mexico were hard pressed to see any priests or get any direction from the church. The groups that formed were called Penitentes, and they would sometimes take their religion to a form that was quite serious, participating in activities such as beating themselves with barbed wire and willows and the like; this was not civilized behavior to the archbishop. They also created their own saints, and paintings that weren't sanctioned by the church so this was all very primitive to archbishop that came in from France. So the building of the cathedral, the attitude of the archbishop, and his alienation of the people created a stigma in the whole area of this church and the archbishop and at the same time the church started harboring negative beliefs about the people. But that was a long time ago and some people had forgotten about it.

Father John just looked at Father Juan as the latter drove on. "But you haven't," said Father John.

"No," said Father Juan. "It's not that simple. It was the politics of the time. There was a lot of bad blood. People were being driven out of the church. Some people were alienated from the church because one man did not want to understand the ways of the Northern Worship. What kind of audacity tells a man he should tear down a building so he can replace it with one that fits his persona?"

For the rest of the ride, the fathers talked about what was happening in Europe; they talked about ego and about the sins of humanity and how people are treated can reflect on a community and influenced by one man.

Father John took mental notes. They were parallels in this world wherein people were insensitive and cloaked their intentions under their clothes; they seemed to be honorable but hid their true intentions.

*   *   *

A couple of months had passed, and the two fathers had solidified their brotherhood of the cloth and of their minds. Father John had forgotten all about changing his name, and Father Juan had found a way to get Prince into the rectory without the monsignor getting too uptight. One day, father Juan had explained to the monsignor that the archdiocese had sent a special message about a concern about mice control, and one of the ways to address the issue was to have a cat on the property. Prince was brought in. The paperwork was drawn up and that took care of that. Father John's cat was in. Father Juan winked at him, and Father John winked back. Father John made the sign of the cross and spoke to God. "Please forgive me, God. I must take care of my grandmother's cat."

*   *   *

Earl Stives was back and forth between Washington, DC, and Santa Fe and would keep the fathers up to date on the news as what was happening on the world front. That association kept a lot of the local politicians very friendly with Father John, which made the monsignor a little suspicious at times.

"Father John, I need you to expedite that building project for us at the city office. It seems that it has taken more time than I thought it would." The monsignor dismissed the father.

Father John walked over to the city office and sat down in the waiting area. The clerk came out and sat down with the father. "Yes, Father John, how can I help you?"

Father John explained, "These are the drawings for the completion of the church's porch in San Isidro, and we haven't received a final approval from your office so that we can go ahead and complete the project. Your name is Martin, right?"

"Yes, Father," Martin replied. "You're a friend of Señor Stives, right?"

Father John looked at him and said, "Yes."

Martin smiled and said, "I'll be right back, Father."

Father John sat there. He folded the drawings back to their original form and placed them back into their envelope.

Martin came back into the room, followed by the mayor. "Father John, it is great to see you!" said Mayor Lujan.

Father John quickly sat up. "Good morning, mayor. I didn't mean to disturb you."

"Disturb me? Don't be silly. You're not disturbing me. Please come into my office." He led Father John into his office.

The father and the mayor both sat down on very comfortable chairs. "Martin has told me that we have been late on some paperwork for the church; rest assured that won't happen again," Mayor Lujan barked.

Father John explained about the final approval process, noting that it was not late.

The mayor was not going to be upstaged. "No, no, we will take care of it," He assured the father. "Can I get you some coffee, a drink perhaps?"

Father John declined.

The mayor was clearly mad. "How is Señor Stives, nowadays?"

Father John replied, "He is fine. He's in Colorado doing some work."

The mayor just took a sip of coffee. Martin walked in the room and handed some papers to the mayor. "This should be the final paperwork for the San Isidro Project," The Mayor said as he handed the paperwork to the father. "Father. Anytime you have something that you want done, you can come to me. You understand."

Father John stood up and shook his hand. "I will remember that." Father John walked out the door, and Martin followed him through the office. Father John looked back.

"Father John?" Martin stopped him at the door. Martin looked at him with great interest and took his hand. "It was great honor to meet you, Father. Father, there is a favor I would like to ask of you?"

Father John smiled and said, "Yes."

"Father, I would like for you to come to my family's for dinner some time."

Father John was elated. It was the first time he'd been invited to someone's house; that was a sign of the community accepting the priest. He was very happy. "Yes, yes!" said the Father.

Father John and Martin made the arrangements.

Father John rushed into the rectory to tell Father Juan. Father Juan and Prince were in the kitchen cleaning up the pantry. "Father Juan, guess what?"

Father turned around. "You've discovered that city hall will not cooperate with the monsignor and the archbishop," said Father Juan, as he wiped the breakfast pots down. Prince meowed and rubbed at father John's legs as he walked in the room.

"No, not really. The mayor stepped in, and the project for San Isidro has been given final approval."

Father Juan turned around as he dropped the pot on the brick floor. The cleaning ladies quickly started to clean up the water that had splattered on the brick floors.

"Is there anything wrong?" asked Father John.

Father Juan just stared at him. "No . . . Nothing is wrong." Prince stared at Father Juan.

Father John walked toward the monsignor's office. The monsignor's office was cluttered with tons of books, it was dark and dingy, and the furniture was cluttered and uninviting. Father John wondered why anyone would keep his office, a place where he had to spend so much to time so dark and gloomy. "Any luck with those imbeciles at city hall?" asked the monsignor.

"Yes, the mayor has given us the final approval for the San Isidro project," said Father John.

The monsignor looked up from what he was doing in amazement. Father John felt that he had done something good, so he just laid the paperwork down on the cluttered desk. Monsignor Dimor inspected the papers. "How in the world did you—?"

Father John interrupted his question. "Do you believe in angels, monsignor?"

"I do, in the academic sense," The monsignor quickly answered.

As Father John turned to leave the office, the monsignor looked up from the papers he was verifying. "By the way," he said, "I will be relocating to Albuquerque now that you have arrived, and you can utilize this office."

Father John had a big smile as he walked down the big hallway toward the kitchen. Prince followed with his tail pointed toward the sky in stride. The monsignor came out of his office, the paperwork in hand, looking at them both.

*   *   *

As the weeks passed, Father John and Father Juan got to spend more time together in the community, as the monsignor communicated from Albuquerque the administrative duties for the archdiocese.

The dinner with Martin and his family went very well, and Father John got to meet many more families in the same community on Canyon Road and Cerro Gordo, on the east end of Santa Fe. The farther you went up the road, the more beautiful it became. The Santa Fe River came down from the ponderosa country and fed the acequias or little rivers and the fields where the families planted corn and beans. The people built their adobe homes connected by coyote cedar fences. Goats and cows grazed in the fields; horse-drawn carts were still being used to move hay into barns. The cottonwood trees embraced the warm, summer breeze, and large clouds formed by rainstorms framed the magnificent mountains, and daily, Father John would appreciate the beauty of it all.

This day, he was on his way to see the Romero family. The Romero's lived on the northeast side. The father enjoyed walking toward that direction in the early morning. Canyon Road was a hard, dirt road; it was one of the roads up toward that direction on one side of the river. There were many houses on both sides but the farther you traveled up, the fewer there were. Father John loved to walk to get his exercise and for the opportunity to meet the people. The majority being Catholic, getting to know his parishioners as a priority for him; the more he walked in that direction, the more families he got to meet. The women would come out and greet him as they did their daily chores or the men would stop their work and talk to him in Spanish; he would answer in broken Spanish, and they loved the effort.

Father Juan kept his ministry closer to town, pretty much with the same passion, and the two fathers would share their stories at night by the table, with Prince listening in. Father Juan would coach father John on his Spanish so that he could handle himself in the neighborhood during the day. They knew that their work was growing, and they were happy that they were making a difference. "You know, it has been very good since you have arrived," said Father Juan.

"Oh?" Father John looked up.

Father Juan was startled when Prince jumped onto his lap. "You and this animal come into town, and things begin to change, I mean, for the better."

Father John corralled Prince. "I thank you for the compliment, Father," He replied.

Father Juan went on to explain that the monsignor was in Albuquerque to expand the cathedral's role to bring in more priests, most likely the Franciscans, which was the original sect who came in with the explorers. That situation might affect the working relationship between them because it might split them up in the future. Father Juan made a face. "That might change the good work that we have done in the last few months. All the gente are really getting pretty comfortable with us, and they are trusting us, and that has not happened in a long time. The monsignor and the archbishop have kept everybody away from the church with their attitude."

"I think there is a reason why things are the way they are, Father Juan," said father John.

Father Juan just looked at him and leaned back in his chair, saying, with a hint of disappointment, "Well, aren't we philosophical tonight?"

Father John looked on at the evening sky, with Prince and Father Juan on the rocking chairs some parishioners had made for them. The sky was brilliant blue with clouds of pink, orange, and gray as the sun sunk into the horizon. They sat and prayed for answers, and Prince stared unto the yard.

*   *   *

In September, the whole community was getting ready for the festivities, Las Fiestas. Father Juan and Helen, the kitchen supervisor filled Father John in on the preparations, as the city crews prepared the plaza. For months, the young men and women of the city competed to fill the roles of Don Diego de Vargas and his conquistadores, and this year, the mayor was to pick the winners. Along with the roles, the pageantry had to reenact the peaceful re-conquest of Santa Fe in the late 1600s. The church was very much a part of the celebration because of the statue that the conquistadores had brought with them. It was the statue of Our Lady of the Virgin Mother of Jesus that protected them through their journey and through what they thought was to be the retaking of the royal city of Santa Fe for the king and queen of Spain. The statue was placed in the Rosario Chapel (a small church on the other side of the hill), and every September from then on, the Catholic community has a holy procession to commemorate their love for and her protection of the citizens of Santa Fe. The procession would take Our Lady from Rosario Chapel to the cathedral and have her on display for the whole weekend. The whole celebration of Las Fiestas is centered on a religious activity and getting the community together of the pueblos and the peoples of Santa Fe. The plaza was decorated with brightly colored lights, and booths were set up to serve food for the participants. Mariachi music, cowboys, horses, and rodeos were set up on vacant grounds, and to wind it up, on Sunday afternoon, was a parade on Palace Avenue where everyone got together to laugh and greet each other. Father John had never seen anything like this—what a happy community, what a happy gathering in the mountains of northern New Mexico, and it had been happening for hundreds of years. Las Fiestas went on for three days, and it was all good.

*   *   *

In Albuquerque, Monsignor Dimor was in the large meeting room with the two other fathers and the representatives from the archdiocese, Archbishop Robert Lanser and Monsignor James Miller. "It seems like Father Smith has a lot of clout in Santa Fe these days, where you couldn't get a chicken coop built." Said one of the fathers. There was laughter around the room. "Laugh it up; I'm going to take advantage of this clout as you call it," said the monsignor. Then laughter ceased.

Archbishop Robert Lanser and his assistant, Monsignor James Miller, met in another room after the meeting. "From everything I've heard, they both are doing a tremendous job in Santa Fe. The community is accepting them with open arms, and the attendance is increasing at the cathedral." Said Monsignor Miller.

The monsignor smiled at the archbishop. "I do not particularly care for our priests playing politics, though. Father Smith immediately came into town and somehow came into power of some sort with the association of a lawyer he met on the train." Said the archbishop cautiously.

"So what's this lawyer's name?" asked the archbishop.

"As I understand it, his name is Earl Stives. He must have connections in Washington, DC, and at the state capital because the governor is very friendly with him as well." "That could be a blessing in disguise for us in Santa Fe. Father John Smith could be that positive figure we need to our building projects in the archdiocese." Said Monsignor Miller.

The archbishop smiled. "I suppose your right." The archbishop said as he looked over his reading glasses.

Monsignor James put his hands on the desk and leaned forward, "You're just not used to someone who is headstrong and can stand up for himself."

Monsignor and the archbishop continued the discussion, but the latter was not pleased with the situation.

The monsignor left the office with an uneasy feeling about the archbishop and his intentions toward Father Smith and Father Juan and the good work they were doing in Santa Fe. Monsignor James had been witness to a few priests who survived by just being robots, silently and without asking for fulfillment of personal needs—would work after he thinks about those who have not withstood the pressure. If the archbishop did not see that you were adhering to his style of relaying the word, he would find a way to get you to fall in line or find a way to have you transferred to some mental institution, but this time, Father John who had a strong friend, an unknown identity from out of town, an ace in the hole. The monsignor's job was to find out who this Earl Stives was and what his influence in Santa Fe was. The archbishop did not want to make a move unless he was sure it wouldn't jeopardize his position.

*   *   *

The world was being threatened by the madman in Europe. The local paper, *The New Mexican*, was reporting that things were getting worse. Europe was being invaded by goose-stepping, fear-mongering, and swastika-bearing soldiers. Innocent people were being subjected to who knows what. Father John's homilies took on personal views on Sunday, and sometimes he asked God for direction. He heard from Earl from time to time.

One day, Earl walked in and asked, "What's for dinner?"

Father John stood up and hugged him.

"Now what's that all about?" asked Earl.

"It's just nice to see you," said the father. "How have you've been? Come have a seat."

Prince ran from the other room and jumped up on Earl's lap.

"Oh, man, look at this guy. Dude, you are huge! What have you been eating?" Prince began to purr and turn around like he was glad to see Earl. "What is he, sixteen pounds or what?"

Father John smiled. Earl hugged Prince. Father and Earl talked about old times. Father Juan joined them, and they all went out to La Fonda and enjoyed a great New Mexican plate of enchiladas, beans, and tortillas. They talked into the night while the Chili Line blew its steam and its whistle, as it puffed all through town and up the hill toward the Española Valley. All the politicians in town paid their homage to the priests and Señor Stives during the dinner. Dinner was free.

Earl updated the fathers on how the U.S Congress was hanging back, not getting involved in the conflict in Europe. Father John's heart sank. "People in Europe are suffering," he said. "Some of the families who helped me get here are suffering."

Earl lit his cigar and said, "There are two thoughts in Congress. Some argue that The Nazis are not our problem and it will go away, and others argue that Hitler will not stop until he conquers not only Europe but England, Russia, and America as well."

Father John took a sip of his coffee. "I'm afraid this man is not concerned just with conquest; he is obsessed with the notion of a purification of a race, his, or what he thinks is his race." Father John went on to tell Earl and Father John what he knew about the Nazi Party.

They were both spellbound, and they almost could not believe what Father John was saying. "That's impossible; they could never pull something like that off," said Earl.

"Let's pray they do not," said Father John.

Earl also let the fathers know that there was going to be some military types meeting with him and the governor about some land west of

Santa Fe that can be easily isolated from the public for future use by the government, something about research and development.

"Oh and I almost forgot." Said Earl.

Earl took notes in a small leather-bound book. Earl had a surprise for the fathers as they sat at the dinner table. He took two envelopes out of his coat pocket.

Both of the fathers read at the same time; they looked at each other, and they could not believe what they read. Father John said, "This cannot be happening, can it?"

Earl sat back and lit his cigar and took a puff. "Yes, my friends, you're both going to meet the president of the United States of America. Now, he is going to be in Colorado Springs, Colorado, and I will be with him." Earl looked his notebook. "I'll let you know when. And the governor will be with us as well. This is a private party, and only a certain number of people are going to be allowed to be there. But, being that you are my friends, well, you made the list."

The fathers just sat there with egos inflated to the ceiling, speechless.

"Another round for the fathers!" shouted Earl. "Oh, another thing before I forget; Father, remember that incident in Detroit?" He leaned forward towards Father John.

The father wiped his mouth and said, "Yes, tell me."

Earl pulled out some papers from his briefcase. "His name is . . . Alfred Foster, at least that is what his freed name is," said Earl.

"Oh my God," said Father John. "Is he all right?"

"I won't be able to say anything until we find out where he is, but at least we've located his last place of employment. Now he was hurt real bad in Detroit. The church did find him, and they took care of him, but then he ran away. I'll find him, though."

Father John was breathing again. Father Juan asked what that was about. After Earl left them Father John took him aside and told him the story about the baggage boy in Detroit. Then they walked back to the rectory that night and said special prayers for him.

*   *   *

The next month, winter rolled in, yielding the snow in the mountains and throughout the City of Holy Faith. That is what Santa Fe means and the wonderful traditions of Christmas in the area were in full glory. In Las Posadas, the families went from house to house on Christmas Eve singing Christmas carols in English and in Spanish re-enacting the night that Jesus was born.

The most beautiful tradition that Father John observed happened on Christmas Eve—the decorating of the adobe buildings with small paper bags, each filled with sand and a small, lit candle, called *farolitos*. Processions of people praying in the night lined the streets, and piles of wood burning on the corners lit the way for the baby Jesus. Those *luminarias* lit the path to the nativity scenes near every church in every community. Every household had folks drop in for posole, beans, and tamales that evening. Father John and Father Juan had so many invites they spent the evening going from one house to the next, blessing babies, giving cheers, giving hugs, and drinking hot cider wine. They were slipping and sliding down the Alameda toward the rectory in the early morning singing up a storm to songs that were not recognizable by early morning. It was the best Christmas Eve for both of them as snowflakes fell slowly through the dark lit streets as they made their way back to the rectory.

Prince watched them sleep in the rectory library as the fire in the kiva fireplace slowly died down. Helen, the housekeeper, covered the priests with blankets. Father John never experienced such a joyous, wonderful time in his life. He laid there, Prince at his side purring and a giant smile on Father John's face.

*   *   *

It was the New Year, and the archbishop was in his office in Albuquerque. Monsignor James walked in and laid some papers on his desk. "I found some information on the lawyer from Washington DC," the monsignor began. "The gentleman is a Mr. Earl Stives and he's a Yale Law School graduate. Comes from a good family, in the Hamptons; his father was associated with many a president, and so is he. He is very influential in Congress, has fought for some of the land grants that were lost in the land rulings and resulting transitions between the United States, Spain, and Mexico. He is a good friend of the governor and is very well liked in practically every village in the state.

"He does have a brother, Sam, who got in trouble with the law—ran with the Dalton Brothers and settled in Pecos. He has a ranch up near San Juan and runs cattle and pretty much stays to himself."

The archbishop scanned the paperwork and looked up at the monsignor. "That's all?"

The monsignor sat down and crossed his leg. "Exactly what are you looking for?"

The archbishop lit a cigar. "This is all information I knew before. I want information that I can use, information I can bring to the table."

"How about this brother of his? What kind of trouble was he in? Let's get more information on him, will you?"

The monsignor watched the archbishop as he took his pills.

*   *   *

Father John was in the cathedral watering the plants inside the altar area. An older gentleman started walking down the center aisle, the old man's boots making an odd creaking sound as he walked. Father John stopped watering. He looked up and smiled.

The old man stood right near him and said, "Hello, Padre. My name is Serefino Sena."

Father John was struck by how sharply the old man was dressed. He had a beautiful red and blue tie on, a white shirt, a shiny vest, and a grand black coat. Father John said, "How can I help you, señor?"

The old man sat down in the pew and stared up at the high ceiling of the cathedral's gothic structure. "You know, Father, this is a magnificent church." Mr. Sena stretched around to look back then forward then back to the father again. "My family was involved in building this church. They broke their backs moving these large stones from Lamy, shaping them, and laying them to build this wonderful place for God and his people."

Father John sat with him and didn't say anything. He just took in the detail of the work that had been done.

Mr. Sena went on, "Look at the close craftsmanship of stonework, the huge pillars. The church was the exact likeness of any in Europe, and it was duplicated here on the other side of the world, here in this beautiful mountain town by a people who had never even seen a cathedral.

"It was Lamy's people that brought in some Italians to help, but they ran off, not all of them, after they showed our fathers what to do. I was just a little boy then . . .

"But I didn't come here to talk to you about this church, Father."

Father John noticed two large gentlemen standing at the back of the cathedral. They were both dressed in black, and they looked like they were on sentry duty. No one else was in the church.

Señor Sena continued, "Padre, the reason I'm here is that I know that Father Martinez and you are doing very well and the people are finally feeling comfortable with you two. This is a good thing. We haven't had that good feeling in a long time. You see, the archbishop is not well liked. He and the monsignor have a condescending attitude. I know that Father Martinez alone could not change things, but you seem to have moved the pendulum over a bit."

Father John responded, "I don't know about that."

Mr. Sena said, "Trust me, you have. Those other two are like the legacy of Archbishop Lamy." Señor Sena leaned back against the pew.

Father John looks at him. "You're the second person who made the comparison. Mr. Sena interrupts the father. "I'm not here to speak about Archbishop Lamy either . . . I want to build a church, or I should say *we* want to build a church."

When Father John heard those words, he could not believe his ears; a chill enveloped his body. The cathedral bells started to ring—one, two, and then three—then stopped for no reason. Mr. Sena just sat there.

Father John stared at him. "A church."

"Yes, a church."

"That is a very big project—"

Mr. Sena interrupted the father again. "Yes, it is a very big project, but, Father, everything has been thought out for years, and we have been waiting for someone like you to arrive and build it for us."

Father John just sat there and stared at Señor Sena. "Someone like me?" he said.

Mr. Sena looked straight ahead and said, "Yes you. We need for you to meet with us up on Canyon Road. You'll see; we have everything all planned and ready to go. But we cannot let the archbishop destroy our plans; we need you to help us complete our dream, of having our own church."

Father John looked at Señor Sena. "I do not know if I am the one who could persuade the archdiocese to allow such an undertaking."

Mr. Sena stood up. Father John remained seated. The two men from the back of the church stepped into the pews behind Father John, and they lifted him up, gently. Mr. Sena looked into the father's eyes. "Do you believe in angels?" he asked.

Father John replied, "Yes, I do. My grandmother is one."

Mr. Sena continued, "An angel named Maria appeared to me one night and told me that someone was coming to help us build our church."

They shook hands. "All right, I'll listen," said Father John.

Mr. Sena's voice echoed in the church. "I'll get back to you on the meeting."

The old man and his entourage left the cathedral. Father John turned around and walked toward the sacristy, where he ran into Father Juan.

"Do you know who that was?" asked Father Juan. "That was Señor Serefino Sena. He is a very powerful person. What did he want?"

"He wants to build a church," said Father John.

"Aye Dios!" exclaimed Father Juan.

"By the way, who rang the bells?" asked Father John.

"I was going asked you. The bell room is locked; no one could have gotten up there," said father Juan.

They looked at each other and then made their way out of the cathedral and into the garden. They stopped to look at the two towers that encased the bells. There was no one up there.

Father John took Father Juan by the arm and said, "We need to talk."

They went back to the rectory, where Prince joined their discussion. Señor Sena was a powerful influence in northern New Mexico and was a distant relative of Father Juan's. Father John was not all surprised; it seemed that everyone around Santa Fe was a distant relative of someone. But these Senas were powerful and rich and were related to the Martinez's who had introduced the printing press to Taos and had been instrumental in establishing the Santa Fe Trail Exchange, which brought textiles into the region from the East Coast. So it seemed that this request to build a church was of a serious nature.

The fathers received word later from the ladies in the kitchen that the meeting was set up in two weeks on a Saturday.

*   *   *

Father John started to reflect seriously on his life so far. He started to meditate and pray in his room late into the night. He would stay late after the masses and ceremonies at the cathedral and ask God to guide him and give him direction as to what do with this request. His sociology background and the readings about the area were not enough for him to take on such a tremendous responsibility. This was not just the challenge of figuring out the personalities of the monsignor and the archbishop, which he had done before in Detroit and had accomplished that with flying colors; this was taking on an establishment that might not appreciate his presence and might quite end his career as a priest. He loved being a priest; his whole life was centered on the thought of making a difference for God through the service of the church.

As soon as he had arrived in the City of Holy Faith—this town at the end of the Rocky Mountains, hidden from the world—he had known that this was where he belonged. The people here had the same dreams as the ones he had left in Europe—the freedom to openly enjoy and express the truth about God and his love for them.

No one on this earth could dictate the truth, because no one other than God knew the truth. Many had spoken the words of prophesy and taken on the testaments. All the books were the same—all the accountabilities were up to us; we were responsible for supporting each other. We had to trust that everyone would do right with each other, or else there would be no respect or dignity in our societies. That was

God's truth. When these things were not done, that is when a man, a neighborhood, a city, a state, a nation, a society failed.

Father John cried in his solitude. He missed his childhood, his parents, and his grandmother, and he wanted to make a difference here with these wonderful people of the east side of Santa Fe. They needed him to be accountable to them, for him to support them; the people needed him to be trustworthy, to give them what he was worth. He made a vow that night that he would make everything right.

*   *   *

Father John had been working on a surprise for Father Juan. A room next to the office that the monsignor occupied, about the same size as the monsignor's office, held only old, useless, obsolete files. Father John was puzzled why Father Juan did not have an office for himself; after all, the father did office work as well, and he would often find Father Juan bent over in the kitchen table doing the paperwork, when he could very well be in a nice place where he could hang his personal belongings. Father Juan had been here for almost ten years, and yet, nothing but his room was set apart for him.

Father John, the ladies in the kitchen, the cleaning help, and the outside help all pitched in, and they created a beautiful office out of that old storage room. They painted walls. They moved huge bookcases to allow the windows to be cleared and open. They scrubbed the wooden floors till they shined. They brought in some paintings that were stored in the church's warehouse to hang. It was a great project that took a week or two. All of them were very tired at the end of the day, when Father Juan came back from visiting some patients at St. Vincent's Hospital. They were all sitting in the kitchen when Father Juan sat down at his usual chair. Helen brought him some coffee.

Father Juan said, "Thank you, Helen. And how was your day?"

Helen said, "We didn't get anything done that you wanted us to do."

Father Juan said, "Oh? That's fine; there's always tomorrow."

Father John asked, "How are the patients?"

"I spoke to the very sick this morning and worked my way through the day to the not so sick," Father Juan told them. "That way, at the end of the day, I don't have to be so compassionate."

"Sounds like a good plan," said Father John.

Father Juan started to do his notes, and Father John said, "Father, we need to show you something down the hall. You'll need to bring your notes."

They all walked down the hall. Then Father John led Father Juan toward the unused door. "Open it," said Father John.

Father Juan slowly opened the door. He walked in and gasped, "Oh my God. What a beautiful office. Who is it?"

"It's yours, my friend," said Father John.

A loud cheer from everyone else echoed down the hallway. Prince rushed in to secure the area and jumped on top of Father Juan's new desk.

Father Juan's face was frozen in amazement. He couldn't believe his eyes. He walked around the room and touched every chair and then his desk.

"What do you think?" asked Father John.

"My office?" Father Juan asked again.

Everyone was still clapping and cheering Father Juan.

"I can't believe this. Thank you. But there was no work order."

Father John was smiling and was walking around the room. "We don't need a work order. Look, this door connects to my office."

Everyone hugged. It was a joyous moment—a moment that, in Father John's mind, should have occurred many years ago.

Father Juan's eye's filled with tears as he hugged everyone in the room. The last person he hugged was Father John. "Thank you, thank you," he said. "You don't how much this means to me." Prince sat there on the desk. Father Juan sat at his chair behind his desk, proud as he could be. "Prince, look at this office. It's beautiful. Look a window; it's beautiful." Declared Father Juan as he put his hand on the desk.

Prince looked out the window with him.

*   *   *

Two weeks had passed. Saturday morning came about with a cold chill in the air. The Sangre de Cristo Mountains were pure white with freshly fallen snow. Father John and Father Juan strolled up Canyon Road, passed the houses, the canales with ice all the way to the ground, and the dogs that barked as the priests made their way up the canyon. The trees were bare, except for the evergreen piñon trees and tall ponderosas. Trails of piñon smoke flowed out of each chimney, bending south as the breeze floated them away. Soon they were at the Rodriguez home.

After they knocked, they were greeted by the man of the house. "Come on in, Padres. Welcome."

The house was full of men from the barrio. The men all stood up to show their respect to the priests. It was a rather large living area. The women were in the kitchen with some food, and they all made their way to the kitchen, where more introductions were made. Children, small, medium, and large, were about. The older children stayed, the other children were instructed to take care of the small children, and everyone got some food and sat down.

Father John insisted on discussing the families first and then focusing on business, which was very comforting for everyone. Coffee was served, everyone ate, and the meeting—attended mostly by the men and older boys—was moved to the living room. Father John had a natural way of facilitating; he would make people feel at ease, and he would make sure that everyone had a chance to say something. In this meeting, the father wasn't sure that the building of a church was a good idea, but he was willing to hear the group's story, and it was chance to meet more people of the barrio.

A young man stood up., "Fathers, my name is Pablo. This is my wife, Claudia. And it's great to have both of you here today. We know that

Señor Sena has asked you to our meeting, and we have here today some, not all, of the people who live up here in this area. There are forty-five people here; eighty-three could not come but will get the word later on when this is over. There are more families up here, about 284 more, and all pretty much will go with what we decide to do and help get this church off the ground." The fire in the kiva fireplace crackled. Pablo talked. Father John looked at all the faces as Pablo went on about the logistics. "We know where we can get the proper mud and hay for the adobes, the sand is nearby, the vigas are up the canyon in the Sangres, and we have the men for the labor."

Father John took a sip of his coffee, which was the best coffee he had ever tasted.

A young, beautiful girl ran across the room with a pot of coffee and poured more coffee in his cup. "My name is Juanita, Father." She smiled and ran back. This group was putting on quite a good public relations campaign.

"Well, what about the money?" asked the father.

"We don't need any stupid money!" said someone from the back.

Pablo returned with, "We have significant funds from Mr. Sena."

"What about land, property? Where are you going to put this church?" asked Father John.

Father Juan jumped in. "The Rodriguez, Catanach, and Sena families have donated all the land we need for a fine church."

"We need plans, an architect, and some drawings," said Father John.

"We don't need a stupid architect!" someone said from the back.

Pablo stepped in. "We do have some help from the folks from the city who will help us in that department, and we do have drawings."

"We certainly need a contractor to oversee the project," said father John.

"We don't need a stupid contractor!" someone said from the back.

"Shut up with that stupid stuff!" someone else said.

Pablo jumped in. "That may be true, but there are very capable men here in this parish who can oversee this project, and besides, with the city monitoring the codes, we can build to standards. I know we can get this church up, Father," said Pablo.

Father John turned to Father Juan, who shook his head, as if to say, why not?

The men in the room were looking into Father John's eyes.

He looked around, and before he knew it, he was asking, "Are we sure this is what we want?"

There was a cheer in the room that could be heard all the way to Albuquerque, and inside of Father John's head was his grandmother's voice—*That's my boy.*

"Let's not cheer yet; there are so many things we will need to think about and plan for. I would like to get with you, Pablo, and select a few people for a meeting to view the site, the plans, and the cost, and we'll get this project on its way," said Father John.

Pablo and a few men approached the father. Pablo spoke. "Father, we have all of that done, and we are prepared to give the presentation to you now."

So the group sat him down; the drawings were brought out on large pages of drawing paper. Men stood across the room so they could stretch the plans out and show the views of the magnificent drawings, all to scale, all to proportion, and all accurate. Father John's eyes scanned the document as if he was gazing at the *Mona Lisa* for the very first time. The vision of this church was in front of him, and he could not believe his own eyes; it represented the wonderful adobe architecture, with proportions that blended with the neighborhood. Father John was amazed at the excitement that filled the room, from the children to the adults; this church as a collective dream of theirs.

The meeting also included a visit to view the site. They all collected their coats and walked outside. The property that was designated for the church was a few yards up the road, on a relatively flat piece of ground a few hundred feet from the river. The rolling hills cradled the site and the crisp winter morning and fresh fallen snow on the ground; it seemed like God's hands were there, displaying the place where the church was to be.

Everyone turned to Father John and Father Juan; and in Father John's head, he could hear his grandmother's voice in her heavy accent—*They need your help.*

They all walked back and forth and paced the dimensions of the drawings. In the cold morning on the field of grass, the group of men planned the foundations and pointed at the ground with excitement. They consulted the plans and looked at the fathers with promise in their eyes and excitement in the souls. Another cheer rang out.

With plans under Father John's arms, he and Father Juan walked down the chilly Alameda toward the rectory. Father John said to Father Juan, "This is going to be a monumental task to get through the archdiocese, not to mention the big M and the big A."

Father Juan started to laugh. "I like that, the Big M and the Big A."

Father Juan opened the door to the hall, and there stood Monsignor Dimor. Father Juan dropped the keys as soon as the door opened.

"Hello, you two."

"Ay, Dios mio!" exclaimed Father Juan.

Father John walked in. "Well, hello, monsignor."

Both fathers took off their coats and handed them off to the ladies who were waiting for them at the doorway.

"Gracias," said father John.

"Your Spanish is improving I see," said the monsignor.

"Well, when in Rome," said Father John.

Helen, the cleaning lady, quickly got the plans from Father John and placed them underneath his coat. Prince followed quickly behind her.

"I did not know you were going to be here this morning, monsignor," said Father John.

"I wanted to speak to you, Father John, alone, if you please." The monsignor stared at Father Juan.

Father Juan just turned around and walked toward the kitchen.

The monsignor turned around and walked the other way, toward his old office.

"Well, you've certainly changed things around." The office was impeccable, as compared to when the monsignor had it. The reference books were in order; the furniture was designed with a sitting area in front of the desk for casual sitting. The office was bright and comfortable. The monsignor sat behind the desk. "You don't mind, do you?" he said.

Father John was about to protest but did not. Father John took his place across the desk in a comfortable chair.

The monsignor looked around. "I didn't realize there was a window there."

A door opened from Father Juan's office, which caught the monsignor by surprise. It was Prince pushing his way through. "I didn't realize there was a door there, either." Said the monsignor.

Father John smiled and said, "The old storage area that was in there was just as big as this office, and now Father Juan has his own office. We just had the men come in and make us a beautiful door."

The monsignor just stared at Prince as the cat sat on the father's lap. "You are very resourceful, Father," he said.

"Thank you," answered Father John.

The monsignor pulled out his briefcase and some papers. "As far as your name goes—"

Father John interrupted, "Actually, monsignor, Smith is fine."

Monsignor Dimor continued, "I was going to say that, if you want me to pursue it, I could."

"No. No. Fine," answered Father John.

The monsignor was visibly flustered and put the papers back into his bag. "I also wanted to talk to you about the other projects that we are going to need for the Santa Fe area. St. Vincent's Hospital is going to ask for our help. Cañada de Los Alamos, the college, and the St. Michael's School all needing funding. You seem to be very well set with the political arena up here and have become so very quickly. I'm very curious as to how that has occurred."

Father John let Prince sit on the table next to him as Prince stared at the monsignor.

"Does that cat have to be here?" asked the monsignor.

"With all due respect, monsignor, this is his office now."

"All right. Why is he looking at me that way?" the monsignor asked.

Father John smiled. "I don't know."

"To get back to your question, sir, I'm just blessed, and I have an angel helping me."

Monsignor seemed annoyed at the answer. "Well, it seems like your angel is very well connected, and that can be good and bad. You might be careful, Father."

"Careful in what way?" asked father John. He continued, "I know that you are referring to my friendship with Mr. Stives, but I assure you that my friendship with him would not ever jeopardize my mission here in Santa Fe or my vows as a priest. He is just a friend. As far as the church is concerned and what we have to do out in the community, the better the relationships we have with the powers that be and the better the associations that we muster, the better we will be able to serve the people of Santa Fe. It is not my fault that Mr. Stives is so well known."

At that moment, Father Juan rushed through the door. "Father John, we need you at the hospital. It's the mayor; he's very sick!"

Prince jumped on the desk toward the monsignor, the monsignor jumped up, and Father John quickly turned toward Father Juan.

"The mayor, he said he only wants you!" said Father Juan.

The monsignor said, "Looks like you're needed, Father. I have to run back to Albuquerque; we'll talk later. I was just here to pick up some of my personal belongings. You are needed—go, go!"

The monsignor gathered his things, exited the office, walked down the hall, pushed through the door and climbed into his car.

Father John followed Father Juan and two of the kitchen ladies went down the hallway toward the other door to the hospital. As soon as they all got to the end of the garden, Father Juan stopped and peered down the long wall at St. Francisco Street then up Palace Street. "Phew, he's gone."

"Who's gone?" asked Father John.

"The monsignor!" said Father Juan.

"You mean there is no mayor at the hospital?"

"No, I'm telling you; you cannot be confronting him that way!" Father Juan said. "I just saved you from being transferred to who knows where!"

Father John just smiled. "Father Juan, I'm not going to get transferred," he said.

Father Juan answered, "You don't know him like I do."

Father John put his arm around Father Juan and they both walked downtown toward Taichert's Store on the plaza. Dan Taichert welcomed both fathers as they walked in the store, and they were both treated to a couple of sodas.

Father John loved the way Father Juan cared for him. "You know, Father Juan, that whole routine was not very good, and I think the monsignor probably could see though it."

Father Juan sat there enjoying his soda. "It doesn't matter; I got you out of there. Hey, Dan, how's your store in Las Vegas?"

Then the conversation switched to the usual—the goods that were being brought in from the East. The Taichert family was Jewish and had good connections on the East Coast. They were bringing in fancy things for the rich and famous; as long as they had money, the family would bring in the trinkets—beautiful chandeliers, furniture made in Europe fit for kings, silver dining sets, rugs from the Orient, and oil paintings for the state buildings—all for the right price. Mr. Taichert and the fathers talked about who and how things were being manipulated in the market place; like all the native pottery, blankets, jewelry, animal skins and the like, were shipped back east for electric goods, pots, pans and weapons.

Father John soaked it all in. If there was a chance for some money to be had, maybe there was some money to be had for a new church. But now there was some concern as to how he could convince the archdiocese in Albuquerque, especially the monsignor and the archbishop, to build this church. Mr. Taichert had some ideas himself about how to generate some funding. Father John was not shy about asking Mr. Taichert, a smart businessman, how to come up with some funds for a new church.

Mr. Taichert just smiled from behind the counter. "Father, I do know some folks who might help get some money together for your church. Have Mr. Stives give me a call sometime, and I'll get him connected with one of my friends."

Father John and Father Juan thanked him for the sodas and went back to the rectory. Father John told Father Juan, as they sat in their offices, "Get a hold of Earl on the phone for me; I'll let him know about what Mr. Taichert said."

Later on that afternoon, Earl called back, and Father John was not in. Earl was to call back.

Mr. Sena's aid contacted Father John, and they were to have lunch the next day. Father John pulled out the plans for the new church and placed them up across his desk. There were not just plans; these plans represented a dream of these people. They wanted to have their own church; they wanted a church that was part of them, not some gothic structure that, to them, represented alienation and discontent. The church's history in New Mexico had been tumultuous. After converting Native Americans into Catholics, the church had left the Spanish settlers alone and disconnected for a long time, and the people adapted the religion, moving toward the practices of the Penitentes. Then with the reintroduction of more priests into the area, after five national flags—those of Spain, Mexico, the Confederate, the Union and the United States—had been flown here, the church subjected the people to some harsh direction. As Father John noticed every Sunday, the parishioners from the eastside had to sit at the back pews in the cathedral because of social, economic and cultural identity. The people felt no connection to the church, their worship as a whole. And thus they lacked connection as a community. Some shared activity or effort would be necessary to bring this community together, and the church had to spearhead that effort. Other communities had accomplished their healing by building their own churches, by resurrecting their own houses of worship, by connecting to God in their own way, not by some dictation of an outside influence that did not even take the time to understand them or even know them. Father John knew his mission, it was clear now. A new church was to be built for the people of Canyon Road and Cerro Gordo. Now the hard work was to convince the archdiocese to accept the project.

A call came in for Father John; it was Earl on the line. The pleasantries were always good; that made Father John smile. The two men discussed the project, the progress on the property, and Prince, of course. There were some updates on some family news in Europe that was not good for the Father, some notes were taken by the father, some ghettos were destroyed no survivors, no word at this time. The father stayed quiet.

Father John inquired about trains, and Earl had no information about them at all and said that he would get back to the father.

The pair moved on to discussing a lighter subject; the president was going to be in Colorado Springs, Colorado, in one month, and both fathers were scheduled to travel with Earl on the train to the meeting. It would be a quick dinner party at a hotel near Fort Carson. All the arrangements had been made; all the father had to do was get permission from the archdiocese and Earl would send him the tickets in a couple of weeks or so.

The father hung up the phone and sat there in his office. Prince came in right on cue. They sat there looking at the mountains. That was what the father felt was the most comforting part of being here in Santa Fe; no matter what was happening in this world, he could always look out any window and gaze at the Sangre de Cristo Mountains and feel peace. He walked into Father Juan's office and confided with him.

*   *   *

The letter came into the desk of the archbishop's office; the archbishop was at his desk when he read it. "Monsignor James!" he screamed at the top of his lungs. "Monsignor James!" You could hear his voice throughout the whole office.

His secretary came running in. "What is wrong?"

"Where's the monsignor? I need him!" yelled the archbishop.

"He is in the other compound, your highness! Calm down." She tried to settle the archbishop back into his desk chair. "I will get him for you. Just sit there. We'll be right back."

In a few minutes, Monsignor James came rushing through the door, sliding on the floor and stopping at the desk of the archbishop. Out of breath, the monsignor collected himself.

"Have you read this?" the archbishop asked him.

"Read what, sir?"

"This request from Santa Fe." The archbishop handed the letter to the monsignor.

The monsignor still out of breath reads the letter and sits down.

"Can you believe this?" said the archbishop. "I should be the one to be meeting the president of the United States!"

Monsignor James couldn't help but smile a bit.

"I don't think this is humorous! Do you think this is funny?" said the archbishop.

"No. I do not," said the monsignor.

"I know what I'm going to do with this request; I'm going to deny it," said the archbishop.

"Why? This is an honor." The monsignor looked at archbishop.

"An honor? This is a slap in my face. He is doing this on purpose."

The monsignor could not believe what he was hearing. At this point, he chose not to argue the point.

*   *   *

Father John and Mr. Sena met and had other meetings with the people up on the east side. This was all necessary for the planning stages to build a new iglesia. This winter was a cold one. The ground was hard as rock.

This night, large snowflakes drifted down from the sky and appeared magically as they passed by the window. Inside the old adobe house, the men of the barrio gathered together to discuss the need for their own church. One of them said, "It will be a church so grand, so beautiful that it will rival any other."

Father John admired his enthusiasm. The wood stove crackled as the meeting got under way. The old house was warm within the adobe walls. The smell of piñon wood draped the room.

"Maybe we should hire a professional, to be sure that it gets done right," Remarked the old man in the corner smoking his pipe.

"Could it be that your brother has the paper that designates him a know-it-all and declares him smarter than the men in this room, who, by the way, taught him everything, he knows!" Felipe barked back at the old man.

That started a whole new round of shouting among the groups at each end of the smoke-filled room.

Father John stood up. "No. This iglesia will be built by its own people. If Waldo wants to help, even though he does not live here, that is fine; we have the help from the mayor's office to get things through." The two men who were arguing stared at each other. The Padre was determined to keep this project in line. "The property was a generous gift by the families up here. We have the land now, and if everything goes well, we could start in March when the snows have melted."

When the padre spoke, the men in the room listened. It was common knowledge that, if you got the Padre mad, that would surely mean that God was not far behind.

"Pablo, along with many in this room, generated these plans, and they represent a beautiful church that will have massive walls to support this beautiful structure. It will be built of mud from la tierra to reach up into the heavens. We will have to have vigas so big that it will take many men to move them." Father John acted as if he was up there on the pulpit already, as he spoke this vision of grandeur. All the men in the room shared his vision on that cold winter night.

The meeting with the archbishop had not been scheduled, and everyone was getting anxious. The plans were to be inspected by a panel, and approval was to be given if everyone from the archdiocese was in agreement. "So, how come they haven't responded?" asked Mr. Sena.

Father John answered, "I have no idea."

"It's been weeks. We're losing time, qué no?" said Mr. Sena.

Father John said, "I called again last week, and he gave me the same answer—that he would get back to me."

*　　*　　*

The archdiocese got a hold of the news that the people on the east side of Santa Fe were planning a new church; the reaction was negative as to be expected.

"That is completely absurd. Nobody can just simply put up a church wherever they want." The archbishop became enraged. "What is Father Smith thinking, that he can just do this without any justification or even permission?"

His assistant, Monsignor James, answered, "Well, according to the charter, Father Smith is in charge up there, and one of his responsibilities is to evaluate the necessity for other churches to be built."

The archbishop, making notes in a wild fashion, retorted, "Well that is something we need to eliminate; this has never come up before."

All over northern New Mexico, there were small adobe iglesias, some so small they were in people's backyards. The archbishop wanted to ensure that that would never occur here, so he called a meeting with Father John and Father Juan.

Monsignor James stood there in sadness as the archbishop had another episode. This time, it wasn't a minor one. The archbishop took on a dark side that scared the monsignor. "I'm going to get this Father Smitzer, Smith, whoever he is! I know what he is after! He is after . . . my position. You are all after my position. You all want to be the archbishop."

Monsignor James just sat the archbishop down. "Please, you need to rest."

*   *   *

The fathers came down from Santa Fe, and they were escorted to the main office of the archbishop. Monsignor Dimor was there, as well as Monsignor James, who was in the room when they both arrived. The staff was very friendly with the fathers from Santa Fe, as if they were heroes of some sort. The young lady who escorted them in stood there in awe of Father John.

"You can leave now," said the archbishop to the staff person.

The room was silent. Father John sat there with his smile. Father Juan squirmed in his seat.

"Well, Father, a new church, is quite an undertaking." The archbishop said raising an eyebrow condescendingly in Father John's direction.

No one answered.

"I see from your submission that all the factors have been addressed. This is a tremendous amount of paperwork. How in the world did this get prepared so quickly?"

Father Juan looked at Father John then he smiled at his friend and focused on the archbishop, "This work has been in the mill for quite a long time. The justification study that I prepared did not take that much time. All the rest of the plans were drawn and set up with guidance from the city planning and engineering departments. The finance portion of the project will be covered by many in the community who have made a commitment to get this done—not only the church but the rectory as well. As you can see, there is a commitment of property."

The archbishop and the monsignors looked over the paperwork. "All of this is quite complete. I'm impressed," said Monsignor James.

The archbishop looked at the monsignor as if his assistant had stabbed him in the back. Minutes passed, and it seemed like an hour. "We will look into it," the archbishop said as he put the paperwork down.

"The folks up there want to start as soon as the snow melts," said father John.

"Well, they are just going to have to wait," shouted the archbishop.

"Your highness," Father John stopped for a moment, trying to catch the archbishop's eyes. When the latter refused to meet his gaze, the father continued in a gentle but firm voice. "I'm just the messenger. These people do not fit in the cathedral in more ways than one; they want their own place to worship, and this is a great opportunity for us to fulfill a dream that they have. Another thing, all the other neighborhoods in Santa Fe have their own churches. These folks up there on the east side feel they have been left out; they feel abandoned. There is a historical connection as well that has to be told."

Monsignor James excused the fathers, and the meeting ended. The archbishop began to stare down at the floor. The fathers walked out and down the hallway.

"Fathers!" shouted Monsignor James.

The fathers turned around.

Monsignor James, remaining in the office doorway said, "Father John, could you do me a favor and verify for me the timing of the Coronado Cuarto Centennial Celebration. If a church can be built by then . . . just do me the favor of looking into that for me, please? And unfortunately—your trip to Colorado Springs for both of you has been turned down. I think, personally, it is a great honor for both of you, but at this time, the archbishop is not in the mood to grant such a trip. I hope that you both understand."

Father John saw in Monsignor James's eyes that the meeting had been cut short for one reason and that the monsignor had asked about the centennial celebration for some other reason.

The fathers got back in the old car. "Huh," said Father Juan.

They had their snacks and headed back to Santa Fe, not knowing the outcome of their presentation. Not a word was said on the way back to Santa Fe. The fathers knew that the meeting had not gone well, but it had not gone badly either. Father Juan knew that with celebration date that could be the conduit for new church but they were both very sad not being able to meet the President.

Word got back to them later on that day that they could proceed with the planning. However, the archbishop would like a meeting with the future parish himself. Both fathers knew that to let that happen would certainly be a disaster.

*   *   *

Several weeks went by, and the fathers had received no word from the archbishop's office. Father John took a call from Mr. Sena, and the men were on the telephone for a while.

When he was through, Father Juan came into his office, and Prince quickly followed. Father Juan started the conversation while brushing Prince down. "Señor Stives left word that he will be here next week,"

Father John responded. "Good, he is helping us with the new church project. I just finished talking to Mr. Sena, and he is not happy that things are not moving as quickly as he would like them to move, but I don't want to push the archbishop too much."

Father Juan kept on brushing Prince; his purring was loud enough to hear all over the office. "Prince, you are sure spoiled," said the father John.

*   *   *

The archdiocese office in Albuquerque was busy this morning, with several fathers from around New Mexico visiting the archbishop. Monsignor James Miller and Monsignor Henry Dimor were entertaining two dignitaries from the Sacred Cross Seminary of New York. The dignitaries were here to discuss either the purchase of some land on which they could build a new seminary for the church in conjunction with St. Michael's College, already in place in Santa Fe, or converting the old tuberculosis hospital into a seminary. They had scheduled the meeting with the archbishop later on this morning and were prepared to discuss these options. The monsignors were serving coffee and cookies and the conversation was on New York's skyline when the archbishop finally walked into the room.

Everyone stood up, and he quickly dismissed them with his hands. "Please, sit down. How's the coffee this morning?"

Everyone agreed that the coffee was fine.

"Good. What's this I hear about the skyline of New York?" The archbishop's ears were like a hawk's, and he could hear conversations as if his survival depended on it.

Monsignor James chimed in and filled the archbishop in on the conversation about the frantic building pace that had occurred in the last years in the city of New York and the amount of money that had poured in to support it.

They all sat and made themselves comfortable, and the staff ladies served them more cookies and coffee and closed the doors, as the archbishop always instructed them to do.

As the doors shut, echoing down the hall, the archbishop asked, "Now tell, what the real gossip is going on in the big city?"

It turned out that the two men, Mr. Scott Rivers and Mr. Norman Hendrix, were old friends of the archbishop, and they *were* there to discuss the seminary, but they also knew each other from childhood. The conversation started out with the three men reminding each other of the silly pranks they used to pull on the neighbors and the grouch who lived down the street from them and how they'd had the time of their lives on Long Island fishing for anything that swam out in the Atlantic. They all laughed like young boys again.

The monsignors laughed along with them, enjoying the archbishop's memories. Monsignor Dimor wondered what had made the archbishop so crusty in his old age.

"Those were the days," said the archbishop as he drank his coffee.

Scott Rivers took a bite of his cookie and asked, "Whatever happen to that pretty little Esther girl you were seeing?"

Immediately, Norman Hendrix hit Scott on his knee, and poor Scott almost choked on his cookie. Norman apologized for Scott's comment.

The comment didn't faze the archbishop. "Oh, that's all right, Norman. I've gotten over that. She was pretty special, probably the reason I went into the seminary."

"I'm sorry," said Scott.

"Now, tell me, what's really happening in New York?" asked the archbishop.

The pair from New York provided mostly updates on family members, but among the political updates they also included was one tidbit that caught the archbishop's attention. Norman was talking about the senator from New Mexico and an individual who was assisting in the preservation of the original Spanish land grants, some man named Earl Stives. The story was that this Stives person was very successful in helping the senator with the grants, but that was not his claim to fame. This guy was truly a national hero of some sort. The president had him on some sort of special assignment.

It seemed that a congressman from New York, Martin Dies, was instrumental in setting up an American German youth program of some kind in the New York area and actually getting funding for the group. The group was called the American Bund and was headed by some character named Fritz Kund, who was making trips to Germany to visit the homeland and Adolf Hitler. This Kund character had created a camp in upstate New York and had actually trained a couple thousand young men to following the doctrine of the Nazi Party and that crazy lunatic in Germany.

Well, this Earl Stives was working undercover for the President and had revealed the intentions of Congressman Dies to join with Kund and start their own Nazi branch party. The congressman and his staff and the whole group in upstate New York were arrested. The president regarded Mr. Stives as a hero.

"Interesting," said the archbishop and abruptly changed the subject. The monsignors looked at each other and sipped their coffee.

The meeting went on as usual. The archbishop never mentioned the business of Mr. Stives to the monsignors.

Later on that evening, the archbishop called Monsignor James into his office. "That was a good meeting today on the seminary," he told the monsignor. "Looks likes we can start a school up there in Santa Fe."

Monsignor James sat down in his usual chair by the window, wondering what kind of mood the archbishop was going to be in tonight.

The archbishop opened up by saying, "Interesting things about Mr. Stives; how about that?"

"Looks like we have a hero in our area."

"Hero my foot!" exclaimed the archbishop. The monsignor looked at the archbishop as he threw his cup of coffee across the room. The cup crashed against a bookcase, where there were priceless pots of Indian pottery that came tumbling down onto the floor. Monsignor James just sat there staring at the archbishop as he threw one of his fits of glory. They usually lasted long until the archbishop ran out of energy or the sedatives kicked in. This time, it was different. The archbishop stood up in a blaze of glory; grabbed his chest; took a deep breath; and with his mouth opened, sat back on his chair.

The monsignor rushed over to him and gazed into his lifeless eyes.

*　　*　　*

Since the funeral, the administration building had been abuzz with gossip as to who was going to be the new archbishop for the archdiocese. The two monsignors in the running were Monsignors James and Dimor.

The secretary received the directive from the regional council by mail and read the announcement to the two monsignors out loud. "It is the council's wish at this time to have Monsignor James C. Miller become the archbishop and take over duties as such in the name of Jesus Christ." She quickly folded the letter and stuffed it back in the envelope with a slight smirk on her face.

The new archbishop turned to Monsignor Dimor and said, "May I have a word with you, in my office, please?"

Monsignor Dimor relinquished his position and stepped on through the doorway. "Monsignor, it is—"

The new archbishop was interrupted. "I'm not going sit here and take a lecture from you. I want a transfer as quickly you can arrange one." Monsignor Dimor said in a defeated manner.

The new archbishop understood what the monsignor was saying or not saying, so he was not going to dignify the monsignor's concerns by carrying the discussion out any further. He simply got up and, walking by the monsignor, he put his hand on Dimor's shoulder and then walked out of the office.

*   *   *

Earl walked down the rectory's hallway and knocked on Father Johns' door.

Father John looked up.

"You got time for a confession, padre?" asked Earl.

Father John smiled. "For you, my friend, anytime."

"I meant for you," said Earl. They both laughed.

"I heard you were coming; it's good to see you," said the father.

"This place is looking good."

They were interrupted by a phone call. It was the new archbishop. He was ready to talk about a new church, and a meeting was to be scheduled.

Earl said he had the papers ready for the land and a letter from Mr. Sena and Mr. Taichert on some funding that could be obtained through a grant. It seemed that the father's angel was at work once again.

That evening, the fathers joined Earl for dinner and mariachi music at La Fonda.

*   *   *

The cathedral's rectory glistened in the moonlit night. The cathedral loomed over the area. The padre and his contingency walked through the fresh snow on the ground. They all looked across the garden at the towering gothic stranger. Some in the group were arguing again about some type of wood they should use for the new church. The rectory's portal glowed in a warm light. The entry led into a glorious landing, and everything was prim and proper. All of them stumped their feet to rid their shoes and boots of snow. The landing led them into a larger room with statues, and as they passed the Virgin Mary, they each touched her feet and made the sign of the Cross. They felt strong now.

The new archbishop and a new aide, Monsignor Robert L. Naiz, two more priests, were holding official-looking papers and rolled up plans. They all were at the head table. Two architects, an engineer, and some other men with fancy suits stood on the side of the table that formed the long portion of the cross.

Father John and Father Juan entered with the barrio's elders. They made their way to the other side of the table, pulled out the large chairs behind the table, and sat down.

They made such a disturbance that the party that was already sitting simply stared at each member of the padre's entourage. There was supposed to be only the father and maybe eight others. It was obvious that the father had not paid attention to the letter. The archbishop's group was surprised at the number of people who had joined them.

Many other men and women filed in and sat against the white walls.

Willie whispered in the padre's ear, "I don't see why these fancy vatos had to get involved. We can do the job as good as they can qué no?"

Father John looked at Willie and, with a comforting gesture, said softly, "I told you; we'll talk to them. We'll convince them."

Willie did not seem so convinced. Willie had been there before—he had been privy to many meetings concerning other matters with other people, many times without the padre's help. The workers from the old barrio had been at this a long time trying to compete with the new town rules and regulations where they were systematically being ruled out of work because of the licensing and documentation that was necessary to officially get work in town. Willie had lost so many times; he was not so positive that this meeting was going to amount to anything but another loss. Willie saw this as more of the same.

The archbishop gave Father John the nod to begin the meeting. They all bowed their heads and the padre spoke of the Holy Spirit who was going to guide these discussions and said that a church would be the product of great compromise. Then Father John made the sign of the Cross. The archbishop and his side of the table looked at each other, and all the men and women who had walked so far in the night were also looking at each other. The padre recalled the initial meetings, where he'd had to convince everyone in the church administration that a new iglesia was needed up the canyon. Testimony had come in from the parishioners that there was an impression that the cathedral downtown was to accommodate the downtown as well as the east side. When more and more families had started to settle on the east side near the mountains and the old goat trails began to take on the look of caminos, the people from the eastside had started to complain that they did not feel they were a part of the cathedral. They felt they were too far away from downtown to be included. They felt they were not being heard when they gathered with the cathedral's congregation. The other villages around the town had their own iglesias, and the people from up the canyon were determined to have their own as well. "So that is the background as to the need of another structure." said Father John.

The padre continued. "Your eminence, monsignor, fathers, ladies and gentlemen, we have come today to get your blessing on the beginnings of our church up on the east edges of the town. There seems to be a dilemma as to whether this new church is necessary and as to who is going to build it."

From the end of the table, Willie muttered, "It is their dilemma. We know we are to get one, and we know who is going to build it."

Sudden hisses and requests for Willie to calm down moved about the room.

Father John looked back at Willie. Willie just returned the padre's gaze and shrugged.

The archbishop interrupted, "Father, we have looked over what you have submitted, and it seems we are not sure of how big a church we need up there. The cathedral is quite sufficient to handle a certain population, and you will not need such a big structure."

"Te dije," responded old man Alberto.

The crowd started to discuss among themselves.

The padre held up his hands and faced his parishioners, and without a word, he calmed them down. The crowd in the room focused on the padre.

He turned his attention back to the panel in front of him. "There are many families up there now, about 284, maybe more, and growing, and many feel that they would like to have their own iglesia and design their own house of God as a part of their devotion to God—a house of the people. Size should not be the determining factor, and as you can see, with the new drawings that Pablo and Olivia drew up for us, we have adjusted the size so that we would not exceed the dimensions of the cathedral and adjusted for future growth."

Everyone from the old barrio clapped as Olivia stood up and bowed.

The padre continued, "The newly submitted plans in front of you follow the acceptable building procedures, as did the original submissions."

The panel of priests and builders shook their heads as they reviewed the blueprints.

"As far as the size, your eminence, many more familias will be moving into the barrio, along the river and on the hillsides," explained the father. "And in no time at all, we will need a grand structure to support the church's directive of having enough pews for the people."

The archbishop gazed from side to side and then back again at the padre. "Well, one of my concerns is the safety."

The crowd mumbled and started to react.

The father raised his hand. "We have in this audience the best in the trades; some of these men have taught the outside builders how to build."

The panel of builders did not like to hear that type of assumption.

"They know how to build the safest of all buildings," said Father John.

The crowd reacted with agreement.

The archbishop looked around the room with amazement as the barrio's representatives took ownership of their project. He was reminded of the villages of past, where all the citizens took accountability and placed themselves on the line for everyone. That support, trust, and energy of the village meant that their way of life was most important.

The rest of the panel was still shuffling the paperwork and shaking their dissent on the whole process.

The padre continued, "These people do know what they want; they want an iglesia that is a part of their own barrio, that looks like their barrio, and that can be a part of their lives. And the best way to make this church a part of their lives is to build it themselves. We ask that we are allowed to *be* the project, not just watch the project."

The panel started to converse amongst itself, and the archbishop dominated the discussion.

Willie came over to the padre. "Are you going to ask about the redero, the altar screen?"

Father John nodded in confirmation.

The archbishop took the plans from one of the priests and peered at the drawings. The builders were looking around the room as if to discourage the crowd.

The archbishop again was amazed at the determination of the parishioners. He stood up and proclaimed, "This community; these people; and you, Father John and Father Juan, have endured many obstacles, with onlookers that do not understand your passion. The land was not there when you started your dream. Now the funds have been donated, and now you have plenty of property. The design was worked out to reflect the original peoples of the area, and I respect that. The whole concept of people building their own church is part of the tradition here in New Mexico. After all, that is the whole meaning of a church—a church is people not a building. So I have come to the conclusion that the people of east Santa Fe will build their own church and have their own church, with some stipulations."

The parishioners and the fathers stood up and cheered with joy. They rejoiced and hugged each other. The rest of the archbishop's panel sat there in disbelief. The monsignor just sat back in his chair with dismay.

The padre stopped and returned his attention to the panel, who were gathering their belongings to leave. The barrio stopped and focused their attention on the padre.

"Your eminence, I do have another request."

The archbishop looked at the padre in amazement.

"You know that redero that originally was made for the old military church in the plaza and that is still in storage at the cathedral? We were thinking that it would make a wonderful piece for the front, above the altar, for our new iglesia. We were wondering if we could have those wonderful pieces of stone so we could place them in the front above the altar."

The archbishop began, "Well I do not know about that, but if you can locate it, you can have it for the new church." He stopped and looked around the room at the faces of the barrio. "Fine, it will be fine; you can have it. We'll make arrangements to have it brought up from wherever it is at."

The other priests on the panel took issue with the archbishop; he just continued to pacify the padre's contingency.

The parishioners gathered around the padre. They knew that the redero would determine the size of their church, and they would build a majestic adobe structure to reflect the intentions of the barrio. In the room, all were happy, and Father Juan was discussing something with the elders in the back. Father John was guarded as he gathered his paperwork from the table. Some of the people were patting him on the back, but the father's attention was on the new archbishop, who was still having his heated discussions with his panel.

Father Juan walked over to Father John, "Qué pasa?"

"I don't know," said Father John. "Looks like Archbishop James pulled a fast one on the panel." Father John was still concerned about the stipulation part of the archbishop's comment, and he was going to have got some sort of clarification on that.

"I bet you are wondering about the stipulation I mentioned," said the archbishop as he walked over to the fathers.

"Yes, thank you, I was just wondering about that."

"We will need a licensed architect and a contractor to oversee the project; however, we will not change the initial drawings or engineering or the scope of what was presented. Locals can work on the site. I think that this will be a wonderful addition to the archdiocese, and you, Father John, will be the supervisor of the building of the church. If this is all right with you two, of course?" As the archbishop said this, he proudly placed his hands on both of the fathers.

"It's fine," said both fathers.

The archbishop smiled, "You fathers have been doing a fantastic job up here in Santa Fe, and I wanted to take the time to tell you both that I appreciate all the efforts that you both have made. Now that we know a new church is being raised, Father John, you will be assigned to it permanently. In addition, we will be bringing in more of the Franciscan sect back to the cathedral.

"And Father Juan, you are going back with me to Albuquerque to serve as my assistant. Your new title will be Monsignor Juan Martinez, all of this at the completion of the new church."

Father Juan's face was frozen.

The archbishop and Father John each hugged him.

"It's about time, don't you think?" said the archbishop. "Oh by the way, Monsignor Dimor will no longer be with the archdiocese. He will transfer back to the East Coast. Thought both of you would like to know."

The fathers just smiled.

That evening, Father John and Father Juan sat in their rockers up in the chambers with Prince, watching the fire in the kiva fireplace. "Pretty exciting day today, my friend," said Father John.

Father Juan, with a frog in his throat, said, "I feel that maybe you have become my angel."

"No, I'm not an angel, but I am very happy that you've finally gotten the recognition you should have had a long time ago. I mean, you've been here as a priest for so long and taken so much grief from those egomaniacs that I think you so should be put up for sainthood."

They both laughed and ate some carne seca left over from the meeting earlier in the evening.

"This jerky is good, no?" asked Father Juan.

Father John asked Father Juan, "Now, why does everyone here ask a question then finish with the word no?"

Father Juan laughed. "That's easy, because in Spanish, we ask qué no, at the end of every question, like, 'You love me, qué no?'"

They both laughed again.

"No, Father John, you are an angel. The minute you stepped off that train in Lamy, something changed. I felt it. Things were going to be different around here. Even Monsignor Dimor said that you brought a feeling of change and he didn't like it. Of course, I loved it. The staff started to feel it too. There was a feeling of hope around here. Just your attitude changed the way we looked at our situation here. Before you arrived, I was considering getting out of the priesthood; I didn't think I was doing any good. The atmosphere around here was negative.

"I prayed every night to God to give me direction, to give to me guidance as to what to do. The church was doing what we were supposed to be doing, but our leadership had no heart, no feeling toward our people, and it manifested itself by not allowing for me to be me. I was being smothered by insensitivity, not only to my needs but to the needs of others around me.

"My grandmother used to make beautiful blankets that kept us warm in the winter. They were patchwork and multicolored. She used to say that all the colors were the key to the warmth, a blanket with only one color was not as warm. She also applied that to society. It takes all colors."

Father John asked, "Is your grandmother alive?"

"No," answered Father Juan.

"She sounds as wise as my grandmother," said Father John.

*   *   *

Earl Stives was with the governor and most of the important state legislators were preparing to have breakfast at El Dorado Hotel in downtown Albuquerque when Archbishop James and his entourage walked into the luxurious dining room and joined the group. The group of men sitting stood up and welcomed them to the table. After prayer, breakfast was served. The men smoked their cigars and discussed politics and Washington, DC. Everyone enjoyed the food, there was laughter, and a level of diplomacy seemed to be reestablished. Afterward, the archbishop and his aides left and insisted on paying for their breakfast.

*   *   *

Father Juan and Father John were in the kitchen with Prince having coffee. Helen was cleaning up, and Prince was nervous for some reason. Father Juan was reading *The New Mexican*. Father John was looking at Prince with curiosity. "What's wrong with him this morning?" he asked.

"Esta con los ojos en las estrellas," said Helen.

Father Juan looked at Prince and started to laugh.

"Si, mira," said Helen.

Both fathers stood up and looked out the window. "What does *los ojos en las estrellas* mean?" asked father John.

Father Juan gave Helen a stare and looked at Father John. "Loosely translated, it means, when a young man is in love his eyes are looking at the stars." he said, making a gesture with his finger toward his eyes and the sky.

"Oh my," said Father John.

"Prince is in love! Do you know if she is a she?" Asked Father John.

They all looked out the window. There she was—a beautiful white cat, parading around the patio, looking for the cat of her dreams. Prince was beside himself. He was at every window, meowing like the feline king he was.

"What do we do?" Helen laughed. "I don't think it's up to us; it is all up to that gato. We need some cats for the ranch, so we'll take her. She's been around for some time. I don't think she belongs to anyone. We'll keep them in the back area, if that is okay, Father." said Helen

Prince was entering another stage of his life; our little cat was growing up.

Archbishop Miller enjoyed spending time with the fathers, and he would come down to Santa Fe whenever he could. The archbishop was a kind man and a great statesman, as he let both the fathers have a hand in naming the new church. They were in Father John's office, Prince sitting on the archbishop's lap—Prince always knew the nice people. "All these names, but which should we decide on?" asked the archbishop. "Father Juan, what do you think?"

Father Juan's eyes lit up and said, "I do believe the struggles of the church in this land have forced the people to do some miraculous acts in the past to keep Christ above it all. There was one priest that he heard about in Mexico who was being held down by the military and could not practice his duties in the name of the church; he had a small boy sneak out and give Holy Communion to the sick. The soldiers discovered the plot and killed both of them. The last words from both were, 'Qué viva, Cristo Rey!' The name should be in Spanish, and in Spanish it is La Iglesia de Jesus Cristo Rey, I think that would be fitting."

The trio sat in silence for a moment.

"Cristo Rey," said Father John. The name hung in the room as if it was meant to be. "I like it.

"It has a ring to it," agreed the archbishop.

At that moment the bells at the cathedral started to ring. The fathers looked at each other. The name of the new church was to be Cristo Rey, Christ the King Church. The archdiocese made the announcement on April 6, 1939. On April 26, the site was to be blessed, and preparations were underway.

*   *   *

An architect was hired, and he introduced himself one day to Father John at the rectory. "Good morning, Father. I'm Mr. John Memm, the architect for the new church up on Canyon Road."

Father John greeted him, "Good morning, Mr. Memm. Have a seat. You need anything? Coffee?"

Father John was impressed with Mr. Memm because the architect did not start talking business right away. He wanted to know about the father; he already knew about the community and about the people. And then he let the father know that he was very knowledgeable about Native American architecture and the blending of the Mexican, as well as the Spanish, influences in the area. He would later meet with the original designer of the drawings and met with her and her brother found out that she had gone out to the Acoma Pueblo near Grants, New Mexico and to other pueblos to duplicate the warmth and earthy design of the church.

Mr. Memm showed the father other buildings he had designed, and one of them was the La Fonda Hotel. Well that settled it. This meeting made Father John feels good about how Cristo Rey Church was going to come out and the final drawings were approved.

The contractor was Mr. Fred Gripper out of Albuquerque; he had a team of men—about twenty or so—who work with him. Now Fred was a tall, rough-looking sort of man who left his manners at home with his wife. He ran his company like a slave train—he paid his employees two dollars a day, and he worked them hard; at least that was what he said when he introduced himself to the fathers at the job site.

Many from the barrio were at the job site when the first introductions took place between the workers. Father John and Father Juan were there to see that all went well. The contractor and his crew drove up Canyon Road in about six or seven trucks. The site was already crowded with trucks from the barrio.

The archbishop, with crowned cap, stood inconspicuously in the middle of the crowd of people and vehicles. At the ceremony—standing with the mayor; the governor; the fathers; and Helen, who stood beside Father John holding Prince—the archbishop blessed the site for the new church, Cristo Rey. "Dear Father in Heaven, we ask you to bless this ground we stand on, that this church, Cristo Rey Church, will stand long and proud forever, to serve as a beacon of truth and a sign of the dedication of the people of this neighborhood to you, our Lord Jesus Christ. Amen." And as the archbishop blessed this wonderful site, the sky was the bluest of blue.

After the blessing, everyone stood around shaking hands until, finally, the crowds began to diminish. Soon, the only people who remained were the workers and the fathers. Father John addressed the group. "We have a big undertaking ahead of us; the construction of the church and rectory will be done together. The teams have been sorted out. Mr. Memm, the architect, has given me enough copies of the plans to hand to Mr. Gripper, and there should be no confusion as to what has to get done. If there are any questions along the way, Mr. Gripper should be here. In addition, there will be a team leader assigned to each team, and I will be here on a daily basis. Father Juan and I will be on site as well to handle any situation that might come up.

The men took the time to talk to each other.

Mr. Gripper wanted to address the group next. Mr. Gripper started out by saying, "All right, this ship is going to sail; it's not going to sink. I'm the admiral, and by God, if one of you screws up, you're gone; you're history! Now, over the next few weeks, we will be clearing, leveling, and making adobes, and then we will be shooting for the foundations, so I don't want anyone to be taking any naps in the middle of the day. I want workers, or hit the road! Thank you, Father." Mr. Gripper walked away.

"Good," said Father John.

Father Juan standing next to Father John said, "To the point, qué no?"

*   *   *

In just a few days, the site became a large, flat piece of ground, and huge mounds of dark dirt started to appear at one end of the property. Large trucks brought sand as well, along with bales of straw. At first, Mr. Gripper was not going to use straw. A big controversy between the workers resulted. I locals refused to make adobes without straw, and a two-day argument between the factions ensued. The fathers had to step in and settle the matter with Mr. Gripper. Straw was going to be added because that was the way it had been done for the last two hundred years and that was that.

Father John walked around, amazed at the process. He had never witnessed this before, and he was totally engaged in watching what the men were doing. Water was brought up from the river, and forms were being made with pine wood, one by fours. The forms created these adobe mud blocks; the ingredients were three parts mud, one part sand, and straw sprinkled throughout. One of the workers told the father that, without the straw, the adobe would be like man without a soul or a human torso without a skeleton; it all made sense.

The father dug in and made adobes with the men. He loved it. They made rows and rows and rows of them. Once the blocks dried in the sun, the men turned them over and dried them some more; then they stood them on their side and let them dry some more, stacked them, and made more. All in all, the contractor calculated, for the size of the project, they were going to need a least 180,000 adobes.

Mr. Gripper walked up to the father. "You really don't need to be doing this," he said. "Let the men work."

Father John's response came easily. "I think that, if I am going be the pastor of the church, then I need to be a part of the making of adobes."

Mr. Gripper rolled his eyes and just walked away.

*   *   *

At Sunday Mass, Father John could barely stand for his homily; he had to be helped up to the pulpit by Father Juan. His sermon started off about adobes and how hard it was to make them and about how the straw was their soul. The father's energy was gone, but he got the message through. He had to be helped off the pulpit afterward. It was the shortest sermon ever heard. After Mass he would sleep with Prince on his side all Sunday afternoon.

*   *   *

After a month or so, Father John took a week off from being at the job site; meanwhile, the work continued. The 100 to 120 men at the job site all pitched in and made nearly 1,200 adobes a day for two months.

On June 15, 1939, the first adobe was laid. The footings were all ready, and the workmen started the walls. The concrete for the massive redero was ready as well. That was a fifteen-by-thirty-two-foot solid base to support the weight of the nine-foot thick wall that was going to be at front of the church facing the people.

Father John had researched that redero, which was originally for the military chapel to be located on the southwest corner of the plaza. It was later moved to the old cathedral, La Parroquia, but when the cathedral was torn down, the redero was stored in an obscure spot behind the eastern apse as part of a museum that also contained Archbishop Lamy's red velvet chair and a number of elaborate vestments. The father had made sure that Archbishop James would follow up on retrieving the redero, which was really a series of separate ones that were connected together, and assigned Father Juan to follow up on that duty.

The roof was of vigas, some of them forty-five feet in length and weighing in at two thousand five hundred pounds with a circumference at their larger end of sixty inches. They were gathered from the forests up north and stripped of their bark with drawknifes.

Father John had straddled the long trees and lent a hand; the men had watched the padre struggle with the process, the sweat running off his head like a stream, his straw hat, falling in the effort. It had taken him all day to do one tree, while the others stripped one every hour.

"Qué pasa, Padre?" one of the workers, taunted as he walked by.

"Nada," said the father, wiping his forehead and continuing his work.

Mr. Gripper walked by. He shook his head and yelled, "Hey, get to work over there!" at some workers, as he wrote something down on his clipboard.

The father jumped when he heard Mr. Gripper yell and held his heart as he tried to collect himself. Mr. Gripper said, "You shouldn't be doing that."

As he walked away, the padre gave Mr. Gripper a dirty look.

The plans called for the church and the rectory to be made at the same time. This meant that a continuous building of 350 feet was to be constructed, and once work started, it progressed rapidly. The father's duties at the cathedral were cut down; Father Juan made sure of that. Father John dragged himself in at night, looking like a regular worker. He would be covered in dust and grime. Prince would sit there and try to make sense of the sight of his master. Father John would sometimes just fall asleep on his chair, with his rosary in his hand, not having the energy to take a bath or a shower.

One morning, at morning prayers, Prince was not answering as usual.

"What's wrong with you this morning?"

Prince just looked at Father John.

"What?" The father looked in the mirror. "Oh my!" The father's nose was bleeding. He took a small towel and wiped away the blood. His right ear was hurting, but he couldn't remember why. During breakfast, he kept on checking his ear.

Helen finally asked the father, "Are you all right, Father?"

The father only responded with, "Yes, I'm all right. My ear is bothering me this morning. It's nothing."

All day, there was a ringing in his ear. Father John wanted to see the progress on the other portion of the church, so he wandered over to the other side of the site. There, he encountered a crowd of workers who, he gathered, were not too happy at all.

"Here comes the padre. Let's ask him whether he thinks it's fair?" said one of them. "Padre, it seems that we get yelled at all day long, and Mr. Gripper's men don't need to do anything at all. They stand around and do nothing. It's been that way since the first day. And that's been for the last few months."

The father was dismayed. He'd noticed this discrepancy of treatment but hadn't realized how deeply it was affecting the men. He'd thought it best not to rock the boat now; he felt badly about having remained silent.

"We're not, Father!" they all shouted.

"I know," The father agreed. "I was watching."

"And what's going to happen is that this project is going to come to a halt, because he is going to complain to the archbishop. Then they'll come down here and they'll investigate, and they'll have to get another contractor. We, in the meantime, will lose time. And what will come of that? Nothing . . . right?" Continued Father John.

"Look, what I suggest is that we have to take this situation as we have it. We are blessed to get this far, to get this church on the way. Let's not lose our focus on what we are doing here. Let's not give up our goal of getting what we wanted all along—this church, qué no? I'll talk to his men and see what happens." Father John gets the men to agree.

All the men agreed and broke up and went back to work.

Mr. Gripper pulled up in his truck and stepped down. "What was that all about?"

The padre looked at him and said, "We gathered for some prayer."

Mr. Gripper snarled at the padre and walked away. "Prayers," he muttered, shaking his head. "Get to work, all of you!"

The windows were set, scaffolds were everywhere, and men seemed to be climbing, hauling mud, laying adobe, and making more mud in a orchestrated chaos; it was a sight to see. Every day, Father John would say a prayer for the men so that no one would get hurt. Lord knew that he couldn't take the time to pray with the men; Mr. Gripper would have a fit.

Earl Stives came in and checked with the project a couple of times and was certainly proud of the father and the neighborhood dream that was becoming a reality. Earl was busier in Washington these days, with the British asking the United States to help them out. The United Kingdom had been deathly afraid of Germany's intention; their prime minister had been sure that an attack was imminent. And his concerns had proved well founded; England had been attacked. Earl had been given a special assignment and would be writing to the father from now on.

Father Juan was busy with the rederos; they were ready and packed, and as soon as the church wall was ready, a team of men would bring them up to the site.

The foundations were deep, and the footers were wide. Trucks brought six box-carloads of cement to support the length of the church proper—155 feet. The nave measured 36 feet (inside) by 104 feet. The transept was 26 feet by 98 feet, and the height of the nave to the split cedar ceiling was 27 feet. Beside the sanctuary and altar were two sacristies, each 32 feet by 32 feet. The average wall thickness was 4 feet, and behind the rederos the wall was 9 feet thick. The massive walls were tied together with three bands of reinforced concrete. The sanctuary was 32 feet high, and the main tower with the cross outside stood 52 feet. The vigas rested on the walls of the church and had five points of suspension from steel girders for each viga. These girders were invisible. The girder above the sanctuary beam weighed five thousand pounds. Under each of these huge beams were four hand-carved corbels; under the immense sanctuary there are eighteen carved corbels, the longest of which measures 7.5 feet. The padre, watching all of this come together, was under a spell.

The ceiling proper was made of split cedar, and the odor was very noticeable. Above the cedar was a four-inch layer of rock wool for insulation. The church was illuminated by indirect sunlight in the ceiling. The workers placed ten floor furnaces, fueled by natural gas. The wood floors, doors, and other appointments of wood such as pews, confessionals, vestments cases, wrought iron light fixtures, and the like were crafted by the boys at the diocesan Lourdes Trades School in Albuquerque.

"Hey, padre, look at me!" proclaimed young Diego as he scurried across the scaffolds finishing up the plastering of the church.

"You be careful!" the padre yelled back.

Father Juan pushed a wheelbarrow and dumped a load of rock.

"You've lost a lot of weight, Father." said father Juan.

"I've never worked so hard in my life, but look, it is beautiful—the most beautiful church in the world." Father John put his hand on his hips to hold his jeans on.

"You've had a lot of bloody noses lately; I think you need to go to the doctor."

Father John ignored Father Juan.

Later on that evening, the two fathers were sitting in their chambers. Prince walked in and made himself comfortable as usual on his blanket that Grandmother had made for him. Seconds after that, two kittens charged in the room and jumped on Prince. I fathers laughed. Prince was a father himself. One kitten looked exactly like Prince with the same markings, and the other was pure white like its mother. The kittens loved their father; they just hugged Prince and jumped all over him. Prince took it in stride.

"Are you going to the doctor or no?" asked Father Juan.

Father John laughed. "Or no?"

"This is serious," stated Father Juan.

"Look, it's just that I've never been in the sun so much. I'm as dark as you now. I'll go to the doctor."

*   *   *

On December 7, 1939, the father was sitting in the church admiring the wonderful view from the middle of the pews. No one was there except for a few workers in the corner doing some finish work.

Mr. Gripper came in the back door and was conducting his usual inspection. "Oh there you are, Padre. I need to talk to you."

Father John always looked forward to having inspiring conversations with that man. "Good morning, Mr. Gripper. How are you?"

"Fine. Look, we have that rock retablo or redero pretty well locked in. As you know, one section broke and there is that middle section we couldn't find. We had a hell of a time—oh, excuse me—I have a stone mason to do the bottom portion if you want."

The father interrupted, "The middle section"

They both walked up to the altar and inspected the area below the redero. The area was blank. It was blocked in and plastered over; something had to be done there.

Mr. Gripper asked, "So who are these folks up here in this redero, Father?"

The father was amazed that Mr. Gripper would ask. He explained that the figures carved on white stone and decorated were impressive representations of various saints, angels, flowers, and human heads, in the manner of certain carvings found in churches in Mexico as well as in Southern Europe. The exact source of the stone was unknown, but several records from the 1760s mention that it was quarried eight leagues northeast of Santa Fe. It was carved by unknown artisans employed by Governor Francisco Antonio Marin de Valle and was to be used in the military chapel being erected in the Santa Fe plaza. The governor was commemorating a visit in 1760 by a bishop visiting Santa Fe.

At the top of the redero was God the Father with a tiara on his head and an orb with a cross in his left hand, signifying sovereignty. His right hand was raised in blessing. This was the common representation of God the Father in Spanish churches. Our Lady of Valvanera was next; this was a depiction of an ancient seated statue of the Madonna and Child now at the shrine of Valvanera in Navarre, Spain. This vision was found in a hollow tree when the Moors were expelled. She was always depicted in a tree or arbor, and both mother and child were crowned. The older statues showed her resting on four eagles, but here, a single eagle was behind her with its head on her right.

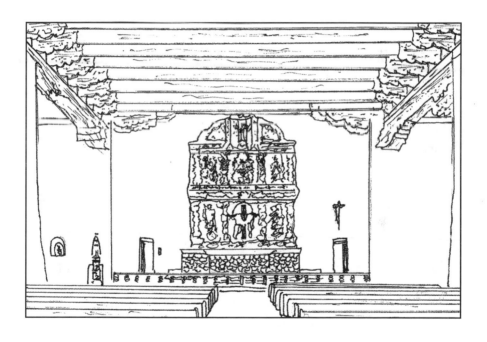

The depiction of Saint Joseph with the infant Jesus in one hand and a flowering staff in the other came from the tale in the Apocrypha in which the suitors eligible for the hand of Mary were called to present their staves at the altar of the temple. Joseph, being old, held back until the high priest made him come forward. His staff immediately burst into flower, a sign that God had chosen him.

Next was St. James the Great, Santiago the apostle, the patron saint of Spain and protector of the highest Spanish military order. He brought Christianity to Spain in the time of the Romans and was martyred in AD 44. His remains were moved in the ninth century to Compostela, a great shrine in Spain. He appeared to armies of Spain many times during battle with the Moors, and their battle cry was "Santiago." Some 155 villages in the new world are named after him.

St. John Nepomuk, the patron of Bohemia and the protector of the Jesuits was born about 1330. He served on the court of the king of Bohemia, where he was confessor to the queen. The king, in a jealous mood, tried to learn from John what the queen had told him during her confessions, but John refused to break the secrecy of the confessional.

Mr. Gripper interrupted, "Attaboy, Johnny!"

When threats and bribes did not work, the king gagged John, tortured him, and had him drowned.

"Oh, no," said Mr. Gripper.

His body was found and buried nearby the Church of the Holy Cross of the Pentitents. Venera Francis from which came the brotherhood of the Penitents (the Penitentes).

St. Ignatius Loyola, the founder of the Society Jesus (the Jesuit Order), was born in 1491 at the castle of Loyola in Spain. He spent his early years at court and as a soldier. Later, while recuperating from a serious battle wound, he converted to God. He was pictured on the redero standing on two globes, holding a standard and a book with a Jesuit motto, *Ad majorem Dei gloriam*.

The panel was the Carving of Our Lady of Light, and this carving was first placed above the entrance to the military chapel (La Castrense), rather than as a part of the retablo. Fray Dominguez, in a visit in 1761, described, "an ordinary oil painting on canvas with a painted figure of Our Lady of Light" as being in the center spot on the retablo. It is obvious that the carving of Our Lady of Light was not made to fit the retablo opening.

St. Francis Solano was the apostle of South America, and the shell in his right hand symbolized baptism. He died in 1610 before he was canonized, only thirty-five years before this retablo was carved.

The two oval tablets at the bottom bore the names of the donors. In English, it is translated to through the devotion of Don Fransisco Antonio Marin del Valle, governor and capitán-general of the province, and of his wife, Dona Maria Ignacia Martinez de Ugarte, in the year of our Lord 1761.

"Thank you," said Mr. Gripper, as he stared up at the stone redero.

Father John guessed he had never even taken the time to look at the figures as they were being placed on the massive wall.

"Thank you," he said again. "My brother was named James. Huh. I know a good stone mason in Albuquerque; he's very expensive though."

Father John responded, "No. I think it is important to have someone from the barrio do this rock work."

Mr. Gripper quickly said, "You are not going find anyone talented enough in Santa Fe to lay stone. It takes a good stone mason, Padre. Well anyway, let me know. I have a lot of workers left here to finish up the rest of the rectory and all." Mr. Gripper walked out.

The father stood up and walked across the sanctuary. He looked back toward the back of the iglesia; it was the most beautiful site he had ever seen. The sun was beaming and the golden light fell through the windows. It gave the father goose bumps. "Angel, I need a stonemason. Help me find one."

*   *   *

The next morning, the father had scheduled a doctor's appointment with Dr. Suhre near the hospital. The examination did not reveal any abnormal conditions, other than he needed to rest more and eat more. The bloody noses, as well as his headaches, were from too much sun exposure. The doctor gave him some aspirin and sent him back to the rectory, where Prince was waiting for him.

"What did the doctor say?" asked Helen.

"I'm fine, just overworked and underpaid."

"Aren't we all?" Helen laughed.

"I'm headed up to the new church, if anyone needs me. Tell Father Juan I'll be up there late." Father John patted Prince on the head.

"As always. Why don't you take Prince with you? He is going to live up there with you soon anyway, qué no?" said Helen.

"That's a good idea." Father John grabbed Prince and put him in a carryall, and with Prince's head sticking out, the father walked out.

The father neared the new rectory. A few men were working and bringing in some windows for the upstairs. The living quarters were beautiful, the living room was huge, the library was fantastic, and the father was already organizing in his mind all his books and manuscripts. He thought of the rectory in Detroit, and this one was going to be his—his thoughts immediately turned to his grandmother, who would have been proud, and how a wonderful a guardian angel she had been. He couldn't believe it had been over three years since she'd been gone.

Prince meowed. Father had forgotten that the cat was in his pack. He let him go. Prince made himself at home and ran down the hallway, scaring a workman in the upstairs room.

"Dios mio!" yelled the man.

"Are you all right?" asked the father.

Ambros came out of the room holding his heart, "Oh my God, Father. I thought it was a skunk!" Prince came out of the room and ran passed the men and into the other room. "Dios mio!" another man exclaims. "I think it's going to be a long day, Father, with that cat around."

Prince seemed to love it. Father loved it too.

Father was painting in the kitchen when Ambros came in at lunch. "The men are sitting outside. You want to join us?"

I'd loved to," said the father.

Helen had prepared a good lunch for the father today; the plan was for him to eats better. He brought his pack and the black lunchbox and, inside, he found a nice sandwich made out of meatloaf. It looked and smelled good. The other men were glad to be with the father.

The father was almost embarrassed with such a good lunch. He was used to bringing simple dried out meat and vegetables, but this was a meal. He asked the other men if any of them would like to have some of his lunch.

Prince had a treat wrapped up in the pack as well. The cat joined the men as well, and they fed Prince too as they talked about the new church. The father asked them about their families, as most were from the barrio.

Mr. Gripper showed up about three-quarters to the hour, timing the men of course. He didn't say a thing because he saw the father sitting there. He drove off.

The father finally asked, "I need a good stonemason to finish off the altar for the church. Anyone know someone?"

Ambros, who was sitting nearby, said, "I know of one. He's working on his house on the hill. He has great skill; he is good stone mason."

"Oh, has he worked on the church?" asked the padre.

"Yes," said Ambros. "But he gets chased off by Mr. Gripper."

"Why?" asked the father.

Ambros answered, "Arturo shows up, but he is deaf, and Mr. Gripper keeps on chasing him off."

"Oh my God," said Father John. "Didn't someone explain to Mr. Gripper that Arturo was a stonemason?"

Ambros answered, "Yes, but Mr. Gripper didn't want him on the site."

Father John was not happy. "After work, can you show me where this man lives? I'd like to meet him."

Father John and Ambros both agreed to see Arturo after work.

After work, Mr. Romero and Father John got in Mr. Romero's truck and drove up the hill. Arturo's home wasn't far from the church. In fact, you could see the church magnificently from where they stopped. They climbed out of the truck. Two men working on a two-room adobe home that was not yet finished. At one end, there was a fireplace made out of stone. The stones in the fireplace had been placed as if they were meant to be there all along, as if nature and not man had placed them there. Father John was taken back. The two men stop working.

Ambros was a good friend of Arturo's and talked to him before he and the father got to the fireplace.

"Father John, this is Arturo and his brother, Manuel. They're building Arturo's house for his family up here," said Ambros.

Father John shook the brothers' hands. "I'm happy to meet you, Arturo, Manuel."

The two smiled and looked around proudly at the beginnings of a new life.

"I was looking at this beautiful work of yours. Did you both do this?" asked Father John.

Manuel answered, "Not me, Father. It's my all brother's doing; he is the master. I'm just the helper. He learned this craft as a boy in Magdalena, New Mexico, from a man who he had helped build churches in El Paso."

Arturo just smiled and watched everyone's lips as they talked.

Father John turned to Arturo and said, "It is beautiful."

Arturo accepted the compliment. "Thank you," he said and shook the father's hand.

The father was taken back. "Oh, you can speak."

Arturo smiled. "Yes. También, en español," he added.

"Yo no puedo hablo muy bueno." Said Father John.

They all laughed.

For the rest of the visit, they talked about the rude reception Arturo had gotten from Mr. Gripper. Father John had had no idea that had happened, and he apologized and made arrangements for Arturo to come down to the church, see the altar, and discuss the type of rock that could be used for the base of the altar. Arturo agreed and said he would be honored; he had always wanted to be a part of the process anyway.

* * *

The next Monday, the padre was talking to the staff in the kitchen at the cathedral facilities when Father Juan came in and sat down with a paper in his hand. "How's the new church coming along?" he asked. "I think I'll go up with you today, if you'll need some help?"

"I always need help," said Father John. "I have a stonemason starting today, and he is going to finish the altar. We went all the way past Rowe in his truck to get the rock I wanted, and we collected it this weekend. We had fun. He is good person, and I've seen his work; it is very beautiful. You'll see. It's going to be flagstone, and I've asked him to lay it flat on its end. It's all my creation. I'm so excited."

Father Juan said, "I've got some paperwork to finish up. Can you wait for me?"

"Yes, take your time. I have a few things to do. Let me know when you're ready. Come on, Prince." Father John exited, heading toward his office.

Later on that morning, the fathers met in the hallway, got in their car, and pulled out of the driveway. When they got close to the church, they saw that there was a commotion near one of the entrances of the church. Mr. Gripper' men and a group of men from the barrio were in a shouting match.

The fathers got off the car and immediately went to quiet down the crowd. "What the matter here?" asked Father John.

A young man spoke up first. "I'm Gibo, Father, and these clowns jumped on Mr. Sanchez and threw him out of the church!"

The whole crowd erupted again, throwing insults at each other.

"All right, all right, stop!" said the padre.

"Who you calling clowns!" someone yelled.

"Stop!" said the father.

Gibo said, "Arturo showed up this morning to work on the altar, and Mr. Gripper's clowns, threw him out!"

And the shouting match started again.

Father John asked Father Juan to handle the crowd. He had suddenly realized that the Mr. Sanchez Gibo was referring to was Arturo, the stonemason, and his heart sank. He had forgotten to tell Mr. Gripper that Arturo was to start this morning. Panic set in.

Father John pulled Gibo to the side. "Where is Arturo?" asked the padre.

Gibo said, "I don't know, padre."

The padre rushed into the church and looked all around the altar. There were tools around, and some flagstone had been laid, but he saw no sign of Arturo. The padre raced outside through the portal. He searched the faces in the crowd, and everyone knew that he was not happy. Father Juan had calmed everyone down by that time.

Father John ran over to the rectory, looking inside to see if Arturo was in there, and again he saw no sign of the stonemason. Father John sat down in the back of the rectory, looking down toward the river. He could not hold back his tears. How could men be so cruel toward other men? He thought of that black boy in Detroit who had handed him that beautiful box for Prince and then got punished for it.

Father John and Father Juan got in their car and continued to look for Arturo everywhere. They looked all day but could not find him.

The next day, the two fathers went up Arturo's building site, where he and his brother were making adobes. Father John got out of the car and approached Manuel.

"I don't think Arturo wants to talk to you, Father."

"Why?" Father John asked.

"He looks pretty bad," said Manuel.

"Oh my God, Arturo, I'm sorry; it was my fault. I did not get a chance to tell Mr. Gripper that you were chosen to be the stonemason," said the father.

Arturo looked up and didn't say anything.

"Please," said the father.

*   *   *

Mr. Gripper's contract was terminated at the end of the week by the archdiocese, as the local workers could handle the finish work anyway.

The work on the altar continued. Arturo; Prince; the padre; and Arturo best friend, Antonio, worked on it. The padre became the helper. It was silent work. The padre had learn the cues from Arturo as to when to get more cement, when to get more filling, and when to get a certain rock. You see, the father found out that, when you build something out of rock, a stonemason doesn't just put any rock just anywhere. He stands there, and some inspiration he receives gives the cue as to where that particular rocks goes or doesn't go; it might just go back into the pile of rock for later. Arturo explained to the father that it was the same with people here on earth; everyone had his or her place, and through inspiration, we are placed here in a certain place to do something, just as these rocks were placed. In the wrong place, neither the people nor the rock would accomplish much, and that placement could be harmful. A person in the wrong place doing the wrong thing could be harmful. If a person has the power to place people in the right place to do the right things that could be considered divine. It was up to the mason and God's inspiration to make sure that the rocks were placed in the right order, in the right time, so they may be the most beautiful of rocks or the most colorful or the strongest, and all together, they formed the most beautiful of all forms.

The father was on his knees when he heard of all this. Of course, Arturo never turned when he was speaking but just kept on working and it all made sense.

Father John tried to pay Arturo for his work, but he refused to accept the money.

It took a week to complete the altar. Prince, Arturo, Antonio, and the father became good friends. At lunch, they discussed the work, and the father came to realize that placing stone on a wall was a work of art. He also learned that the cement that held the stones together was crucial in holding the artwork together and that there were life lessons this man was sharing with him.

After work on the site, the padre would sit in the north portal of the rectory and enjoy the view of the river, the sounds of the birds, and the smells of spring in Santa Fe. He could hear the children playing near the springs of the acequia, the mothers calling them in for supper.

Father Juan would join him in the evening and they would sit and laugh at the old times. "This is good," said Father Juan. "Smell that?"

Father John asked, "The fresh air?"

"Not just fresh air, Padre," Father Juan said lovingly. "The fresh air here in northern New Mexico is," and he took another breath, "the way God smells."

Father John smiled.

*   *   *

On June 27, 1940, a great celebration was held at the church—the memorial of the Coronado Cuarto Centennial. Amid much color and ceremony, Cristo Rey was solemnly dedicated, and the archdiocese also named another auxiliary bishop pastor, leaving Father John as assistant pastor.

Six little baby girls from the barrio were baptized that Sunday; one of them was Arturo's.

Cristo Rey Church Gilbert Sandez
'08

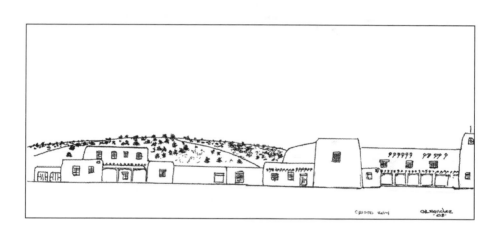

CRISTO REY

As the years passed, the church remained standing. A school had been added and a gymnasium passing a movie house on Sundays. Arturo came by and made beautiful rock walls for the school, the gym, and the rectory. He and his last son created a turquoise patio for the rectory's front yard. Cristo Rey Church withstood time with births, baptisms, confirmations, first Holy Communions, graduations, wars, marriages, and deaths.

And in time, Monsignor Smith enjoyed his time at his church. He earned his master's degree at St. Michael's College in social studies. In the fifties, the monsignor watched his parish children grow up in the era of sock hops in the gym; he was exhilarated by the opportunity to allow teenagers to have innocent fun with music and dancing the night away in the gym to the music rock and roll because he understood them.

In the early sixties, he walked up and down the pews as he conducted his sermons. He had the children sit in the front during Sunday Mass, and he would ask questions about the gospel to see if they were listening. It was holy terror if you didn't know the answer in front of your parents. He would point to you, and beads of sweat would pour down your head until the answer came blurting out like you'd just been stuck with a pin. Then all was well until next Sunday.

Monsignor Smith, as far as the parish was concerned, was always concerned about people. He devoted his life to them, never ever changing his focus. Once this church was built, he and Prince, the cat, forever dedicated their time and energy to his parish. If there was an activity near or around Cristo Rey, Monsignor Smith was sure to be involved. From baptisms to raisings houses to card games to graduation parties, the man, the cloth, the symbol, was a part of the barrio, the neighborhood. You could always see him and his cat walking down the dirt roads to his next visit.

Prince died one night in his sleep. He was twelve years old. That day was a long day for the monsignor. Cleo, his housekeeper came in one day with new cat, one of Prince's sons. His name was Dude. Dude acted the same way his father had and did the same things. He took over Prince's duties at the rectory.

Monsignor Juan Martinez and Archbishop James served the archdiocese well. They both understood what had been missing in the past. Multicultural collaboration, diversity, the simple power of listening, and the exchange of ideas started to move the administration forward.

Monsignor Juan died in a car crash one evening in Albuquerque. He was driving to the hospital. A big truck was going too fast, and the car the monsignor was in was smashed in on the driver's side. That day, too, was a long one for the monsignor.

Earl Stives continued to work in and out of Washington, DC, and he wrote back and forth with the father several times for years. Then, for no reason, the letters stopped. Father John tried to locate Earl's brother, Sam, up near Glorieta, but the Dalton Brothers didn't know what had happened to him. He had just disappeared one day as well. Father John wrote to the last known government office that Earl had worked for and demanded some answers.

One day, he got an official letter from the Department of Secret Service. It read:

Dear Monsignor John Smith,

We regret to inform you that Mr. Earl Stives did pass away in the service of his country. He is considered a hero and was awarded a Legion Medal of Honor, the highest medal given to any civilian by the president of the United States of America. His body was buried in the nation's National Cemetery. We were not informed of any family members at the time of his death. We apologize for any inconvenience this might have caused you or your family.

Another long day passed for the monsignor as he sat with Dude in his chair looking at the mountains—so many friends, so many memories.

One day, in the winter of 1963, Monsignor Smith was walking across the kitchen of the rectory. The doorbell rang. It was a Wednesday afternoon, and Cleo answered the living room door. The monsignor could not recognize the voices; his memory being challenge. Dude, the cat, though getting old, was getting ready to go with the monsignor to check out who was here. The monsignor collected his coffee and walked down the hallway; Dude followed in stride.

Cleo met him at doorway. "I don't know these people, monsignor."

He proceeded to the living room. "Good afternoon. I'm Monsignor Smith. How can I help you?" He extended his hand.

There in front of him were an elderly black couple and a young black boy.

"Please have a seat," said the monsignor. They all sat down. The furnishings were comfortable and warm. "Make yourselves at home, please." Dude sat down in front of the monsignor. "This is Dude. He's actually Dude the third; maybe, I've lost count. I've had so many; they all have been black and white exactly like him—tuxedos."

Cleo walked in with refreshments.

The older gentleman introduced himself as Mr. Benjamin Walker from Little Rock, Arkansas, and this was his sister-in-law, Marleen Foster, and her great-grandson, Isaac Wilson. They were just passing through on their way to California. But they had come by to meet with the famous Monsignor Smith.

Monsignor Smith started to say, "Well I'm afraid I'm not very famous—"

But Mr. Walker interrupted the monsignor. "Oh, yes you are. To our family, you are an angel. You see, many years ago, you saw fit to make sure that this young man's great-grandfather was taken care of. And he pointed to the young black boy standing in front the Monsignor. There was this man named Earl Stives, who made arrangements to locate him. I don't know how he did it, but he finally found Alfred working in the rail yards in Ohio. And Mr. Stives had him cleaned up, learned up, and sent to some schools in the East. Yes, sir, Mr. Stives and a group of men from Washington, DC, were pushing to get Alfred Foster into the ranks of Yale. They never did get him into Yale, but they did get him into the University of Pennsylvania in Philadelphia, where he got a degree in medicine, all because of you."

There was a tear in the Monsignor's eye.

Monsignor Smith asked, "So, whatever happened to him?"

At that moment, an elderly black man walked in the door. "Hello, monsignor, I'm Dr. Alfred Foster."

Dude stood up and looked at the distinguished-looking man at the door. The monsignor, with tears in his eyes, stood up and hugged the man. This Dr. Alfred Foster was the little boy who had handed the wooden box to the father so many years before. The two men hugged for a long time. They sat and looked each other, and the monsignor was so happy to see him.

They all had dinner that night and caught up with each other. The monsignor gave his visitors a tour of the church; he was so proud of everything and of the doctor. The visitors left that night, and the monsignor walked back to the rectory and spent the night thinking and looking up at the Sangre de Cristo Mountains. He thanked God that he had been given this assignment so long ago.

*   *   *

One Sunday, the monsignor had to say something about this world. He was moved by the death of the young John F. Kennedy, the president of the United States. Everyone in the church was somber that morning; he stood up behind the pulpit reflected on reality—the creativity of man and the cruelty of man. He recalled the young black boy who had helped him a long time ago on a train, providing the monsignor with a box that was at the corner of the alter. He told his parishioners how that young boy had been beaten to a pulp on a station platform in Detroit and how there had been nothing he could do to stop it. He talked of how empty he had felt inside. He spoke of a man whose courage had led him to fight for the rights of others in the state of New Mexico.

Then the monsignor told the congregation about a young man who had taught him the wisdom of rock work as they'd worked together on the altar in the church and how that young man had been beaten up because he was not supposed to be here—because he was different; because he was deaf, he was treated differently because he was less than and how much wisdom that man had, if only people would of listened to him.

The monsignor spoke to the people that morning, but it was really the spirit that was speaking to them. "All of us, each of us, have choices every second of our day to be what God want us to be. He sent his son in human form to save all of us, not just the chosen ones, all of us, to die for us—Jews, Buddhists, Muslims, Christians, Hindus, atheists, everyone.

"If you study the earliest written documents of man, we are all the sons of Abraham and all the documents speak toward one theme—to love one another. All the great messiahs speak the same theme—love. So why is man bent on taking that one second and choosing to be the devil's advocate instead of, if that one second, choosing to be good and love one another. It comes down to that simple question.

"We have to start, to take that first step, by asking one simple question: Why do we choose the negative way? When we see those people who are different from us—different in their color, their hair, their dress, their walk, their style, their clothing, their form, their presence—why can't we remember that they are our brothers and sisters. They are our family. Regardless of what our perception of them may be, they are what we are—God's children. It's that simple. It's in that one second that you can choose to lovingly accept that individual. It's that simple, qué no?"

Everyone in the church was quiet and listened to every word the monsignor said.

"This homily of mine is really sounding very simplistic," he continued. "But it's the truth, and the truth doesn't have to be so complicated. I had a cat for so many years, as many of you know. I lost him some years ago now, and I have since had his son and his son's son, and it seems like all of them are one in the same. The point I'm trying to make is that these cats of mine are very simplistic in nature. They have certain needs. They eat, they have their territory, they have their own time, they have their own needs, they tell you when they want to be loved, and they pretty much are independent. They were all the black and white tuxedo cats, regal, and they each ruled the house. They gave unconditional love, no matter what. As long you love them, they love you. How simple is that, qué no?

"Even animals feel that simple exchange of love, animals. I've been analyzing humankind since my college days, and it puzzles me that, at one end of the spectrum, humanity can produce such beautiful creations as music, architecture, paintings, and medicine, and at the other end, reaction to treachery. If only those would have chosen to take that one second to do good instead of evil, this world would be in a better place.

"It is really up to each of us to go out and be that one person, every day, to take that one second and be that one person—to decide to love rather than to hate. We as human beings affect everyone we come into contact with in our lives. That is a powerful fact. As children, we are pure in thought because our thoughts have not been contaminated. As adults, we become affected by our environment. Think about it. If you are a loving human being, how are you affecting everyone around you—your children, your neighbors, your coworkers, your parents. If you are a hateful human being, how are affecting everyone around you? Are your attitudes destroying someone's life and you are not even aware that you are doing so? And how are you being accountable to God by your ways? If an animal cannot be near you, then how can humans stand you? It is very simple. Choose love or hate, one second at a time.

"These rocks on this altar are so different, yet they all complement each other to make this beautiful altar. They all do their own specific job to hold up this massive redero or altar screen, so that all of us can worship every day here at Cristo Rey Church. But none of these rocks *alone*, you see, could create the beauty of the altar. So are we as people—alone we are insignificant, but when we are together, we help each other. We become beautiful, powerful tapestries, and we cannot be broken. Christ reminds us of this when we gather together to think of him. Love gives us strength, as this altar gives us a symbol of beauty and unity."

The monsignor made everyone think hard that day about which choices they were making as human beings and how they related to one another.

In 1964, the monsignor died and was buried behind the church of Cristo Rey. That is what he wanted. The church stands today as a monument of his dedication to the people of the east side of Santa Fe and the hard work of the 120 people that put up 180,000 adobes in 13 months for the soul of this community.

This story is fiction; however, the building of the church is a true story. The passion to build the church was true, and many stories as to how it was built have been handed down.

In 2011, the parish is holding strong and Santa Fe has grown west and south. The school is not a parish school; in its place, the archdiocese has created a larger regional school. The gym is only used for special occasions. The demographics of the city have changed completely. The east side of Santa Fe has changed to an exclusive multimillion dollar area of adobe homes, where no one can afford to buy land, much less own their homes.

The parish of Cristo Rey is comprised of older folks, and the younger generation cannot afford to live here, so they sell out and move. The church, the rectory, the gym, and the school, in the meantime, are getting older, and are a challenge to keep up. The archdioceses have left it to us our small parish to fend for ourselves and raise money to rectify these conditions. The parish is getting smaller and smaller. We fight now as a parish to raise money so we can keep the buildings up, and we rent the school to other schools to keep it alive. Cristo Rey Church is the largest single adobe structure in this hemisphere, comprised of 180,000 adobes, which was constructed in thirteen months, by 120 men and women. It is Santa Fe's crown jewel and should be recognized as such.

Gil Sanchez

My father was the stonemason, and every time I'm in Mass, I see the rocks in the altar and I remember him. And I am proud that he was my father. In the fifties, he built the wall around the school and donated the work, wanted money only for the material. He and the other hundred or so workers never got recognition for their work.

He didn't attend Mass much, and he had a rough life. He and my mother raised six children. Living in his silence, he didn't view the world as others did. My mother had a rough life with him but stood with us and raised us the best she could. She cleaned homes and studied nursing and we all survived. My father found his way to his own light, and he gave himself back to us, the greatest gift any man could give to any child, grandchildren, or great-grandchildren he gave us his wisdom and the alter to reflect on.

The following list, given to me by one of the survivors, includes the names of the workers who worked on the church of Cristo Rey:

Manuel Abeyta	Sam Bach	Antonio Benavidez	Pablo Barbero
Abundio Armijo, Sr.	Juan Barela	Tony Benavidez	Manuel Bermudiz
Jimmy Armijo	Dan Baca	Frank Barbero	Vicente Brito
Willie Brown	E. Chavez	Vicente Delora	R. Dominguez
George Cardenas	Fernando Chavez	Willie Dean	C. Duran
Cruz Carrillo	Martin Chavez	Manuel Dimas	Jose Delgado
E. Encinias	Frank Garcia	B. Garcia	Linda J. Grill
Ray Freelove	Alfonso Garcia	F. Garcia	Manuel Gonzales
John Geanardi	George Garcia	Fred Grill	Arturo Hernandez
Saturino Herandez	Robert Kissem	Ralph Moehn	A. Martinez
Antonio Jimenez	S. Lobato	R. Martinez	Lorenzo Medina

Hipolito Jimenez	Bill Lamareux	T. Martinez	J. Miller
Christina Galbadon	Tomas Medrano	Luis Moya,	Manuel Montoya
Charles Miller	Manuel Medrano	Concepcion Moya	J. Montoya
Andres Medrano	Salvador Montano	David Montoya	F. Montoya
L. Montoya	Luis Montoya	Jr. Michael	Muniz W. Ortiz
Daniel Montoya	Tony Montoya	Frank Muniz	Gavino Ortega
Samuel Montoya	Moses Muniz	O. Muniz	Epiminio Ortega
Frank Ortega	Frank Padilla	A. Pettini	Albino Portillo
Eustaquio Padilla Sr.	Valentin Padilla	Claudio Pino	Matias Portillo
Eustaquio Padilla Jr.	E. Perry	Horacio Pino	Elias Rodriguez
Eliseo Rodriguez	V. Rodriguez	B. Romero	Porfirio Romero
Federico Rodriguez	Juan M. Rodriguez	Santiago Romero	Jose Roybal
Genaro Rodriguez	Ambrosio Romero Jr.	Cruz Romero	Lucrecio Roybal
Roy Rotunno	Eloy Ruiz	Tomas Sena Jr.	Elizardo Sanchez
Meregildo Ruiz	Tomas Ruiz	Tomas Sena Sr.	Mike Saiz
F. Ruiz	Roberto Sena	Arturo M. Sanchez	Lucas Sena
Ernesto Sandoval	Manuel Sandoval	B. Suazo	Alfonso Trujillo
J. Sandoval	Eloy Sandoval	C. Suazo	Lorenzo Terrazas
Roberto Sandoval	A. Sisneros	H. Shields	Santos Urban
Celestino Urban	Fred Wagner	Filiberto Carrillo	Remigo Garcia
Antonio Vigil	Emilio Wagner	Adolfo Romero	
Cruz Vigil	Alfonso Abeyta	Fortino Martinez	

About the Author

Born and raised in Santa Fe, New Mexico, Gil J. Sanchez has BA degree from the College of Santa Fe. Has spent the last 30 years in corporate sales and served 20 years with the New Mexico National Guard as a Legal Specialist. He is the 8th generation in New Mexico and loves Southwest History.

He has served many community boards: coached little league, YAFL, Babe Ruth, Church Finance Board, City Police Review Board, martial arts Kaju-Kempo, Santa Fe Rape and Trauma Treatment Center Board Member, Santa Fe Mountain Board Member, Santa Fe Leadership Director and Board Member, Santa Fe Jaycees, Trained Palace of the Governor Museum Docent.

About the Book

The challenges of breaking down the barriers of a new environment were nothing new to the new priest; after all, he believed in angels. But he had been assigned to Santa Fe, New Mexico. Now where in the world was that? Nothing in the rectory library had any information about the Southwest. This was going to be quite the adventure. Nothing in his sociology classes had any material on prewar northern New Mexico chili-tortilla society. But he would soon find out. His new mission and a new life gave him the colors he needed.